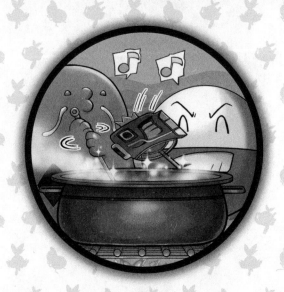

Hidenori Kusaka

I've completed the Isle of Armor Pokédex! I captured all 211 Pokémon to reach my goal. I played through it twice since I wanted both the Single Strike Style and Rapid Strike Style of Urshifu, so it was quite a hefty amount of game to play. I like the Rapid Strike Style more. Which one do you like?

Satoshi Yamamoto

What I like best about *Pokémon: Sword & Shield*: ⑤ Sordward, Shielbert, Klara, Avery, Peony, and the Diglett on the Isle of Armor all have such funny lines!

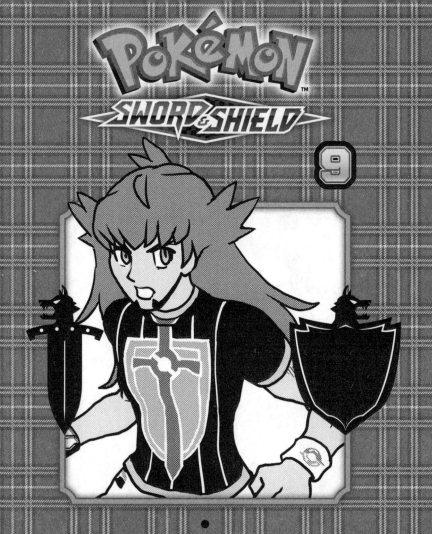

STORY
Hidenori Kusaka

ART
Satoshi Yamamoto

Henry
SWORD

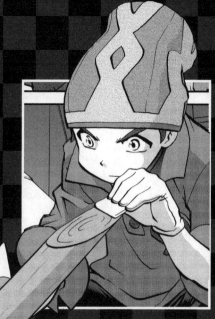

THE DESCENDANT OF A RENOWNED SWORDSMITH, HENRY IS AN ARTISAN WHO FIXES AND IMPROVES POKÉMON GEAR.

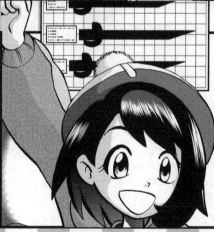

Casey
SHIELD

AN ELITE HACKER AND COMPUTER TECH WHO CAN ACCESS ANY DATA SHE WANTS. SHE'S PROFESSOR MAGNOLIA'S ASSISTANT AND IS THE TEAM ANALYST.

The Story So Far

UPON ARRIVING IN THE GALAR REGION, MARVIN SEES A DYNAMAXED POKÉMON AND FALLS OFF A CLIFF! HE IS SAVED BY HENRY SWORD AND CASEY SHIELD AND JOINS THEM ON THEIR JOURNEY TO COMPLETE THEIR GYM CHALLENGE AND DISCOVER THE SECRET OF DYNAMAXING WITH PROFESSOR MAGNOLIA. RECENTLY, TWO STRANGE TRAINERS APPEARED. THEY SEEM TO HAVE A CONNECTION WITH CHAIRMAN ROSE, BUT WHAT COULD THEY BE AFTER? AND WHAT WILL HAPPEN WHEN THE DARKEST DAY IS UNLEASHED UPON GALAR?!

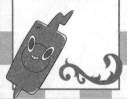

● **Marvin**

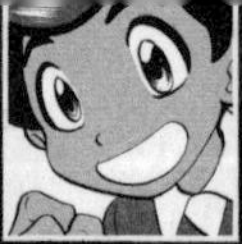

A ROOKIE TRAINER WHO MOVED TO GALAR. HE WORKS WITH HENRY TO LEARN ABOUT THE REGION.

● **Professor Magnolia**

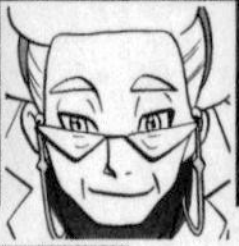

A FAMED RESEARCHER WHO STUDIES "DYNAMAXING," A.K.A. THE GIGANTIFICATION OF POKÉMON. SHE IS A GENTLE SOUL WHO IS FOND OF DRINKING TEA.

● **Leon**

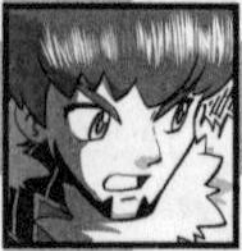

LEON IS THE BEST TRAINER IN GALAR. HE'S THE UNDEFEATED CHAMPION!

● **Sonia**

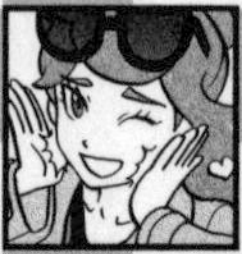

PROFESSOR MAGNOLIA'S GRAND-DAUGHTER AND LEON'S CHILDHOOD FRIEND. SHE'S BEEN RESEARCHING THE GALAR LEGEND.

● **Hop**

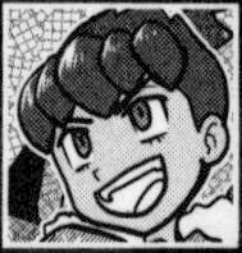

LEON'S YOUNGER BROTHER. HE RESPECTS HIS STRONG BROTHER AND TAKES PART IN THE GYM CHALLENGE.

● **Bede**

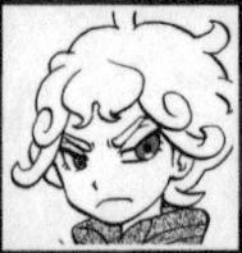

A DISQUALIFIED GYM CHALLENGER WHO WAS LATER RECRUITED TO BE A GYM LEADER.

● **Sordward & Shielbert**

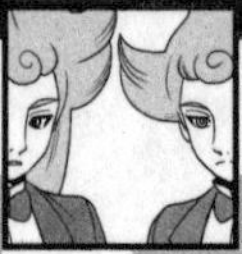

STRANGE BROTHERS WHO ARE ENEMIES OF HENRY AND HIS FRIENDS. THEY CLAIM TO BE DESCENDANTS OF ROYALTY AND HAVE LAUNCHED AN ATTACK!

● **Rose**

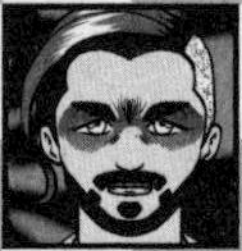

THE CHAIRMAN OF THE POKÉMON LEAGUE AND PRESIDENT OF MACRO COSMOS. HE HAS A DIABOLICAL SCHEME UP HIS SLEEVE!

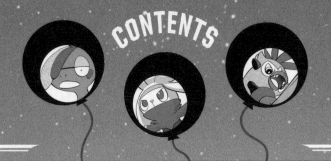

CONTENTS

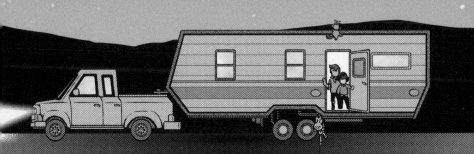

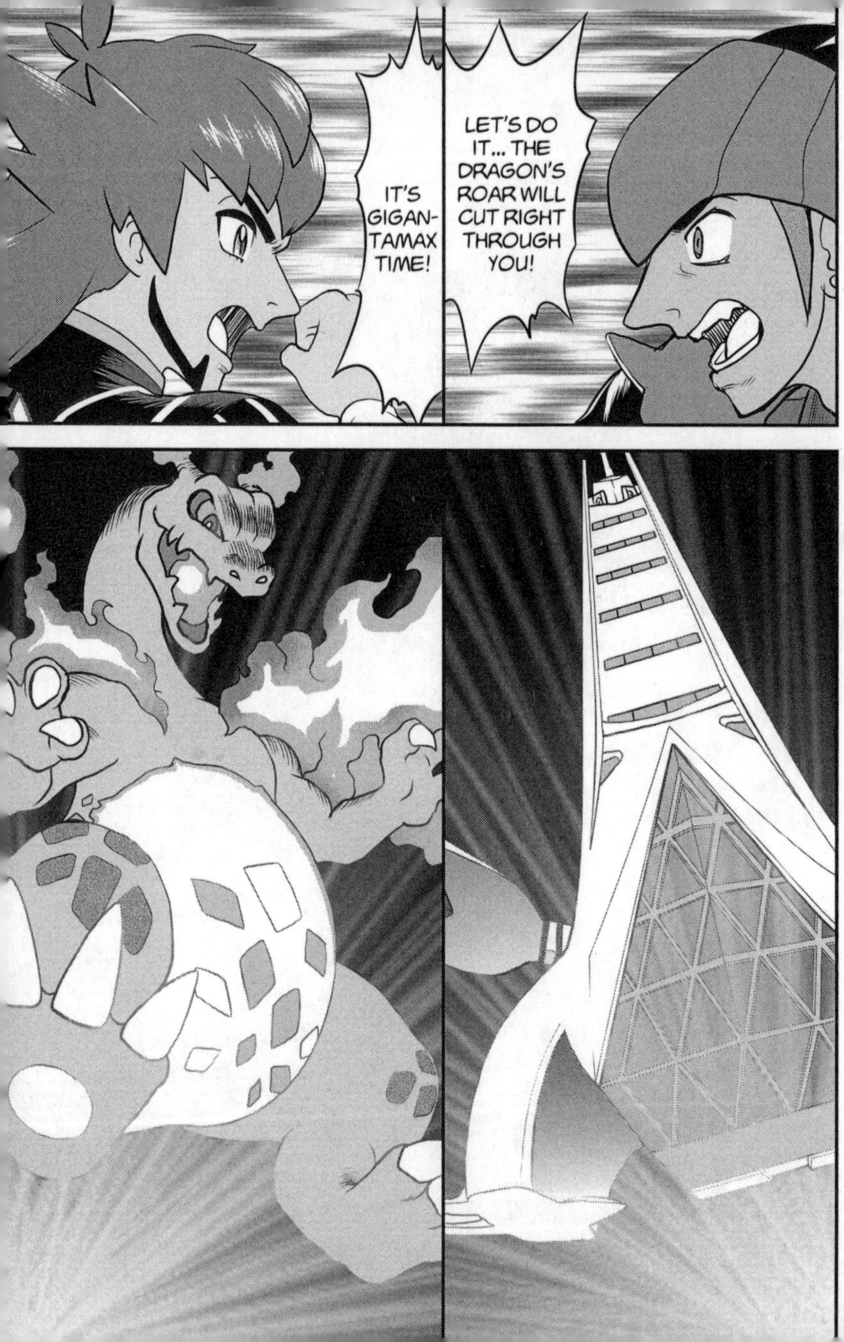
LET'S DO IT... THE DRAGON'S ROAR WILL CUT RIGHT THROUGH YOU!
IT'S GIGANTAMAX TIME!

Adventure 26 Crack!! The Rusted Sword and Shield

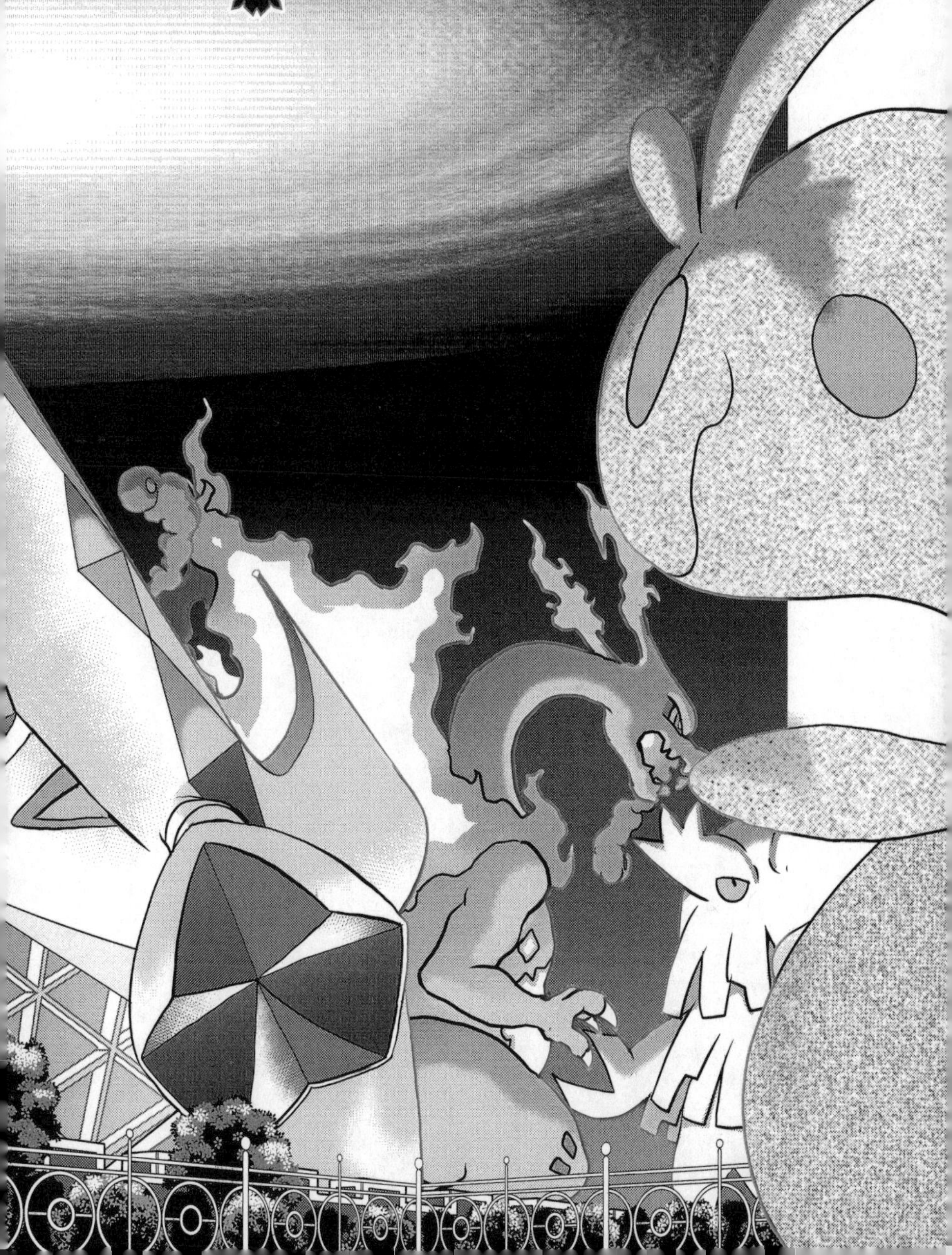

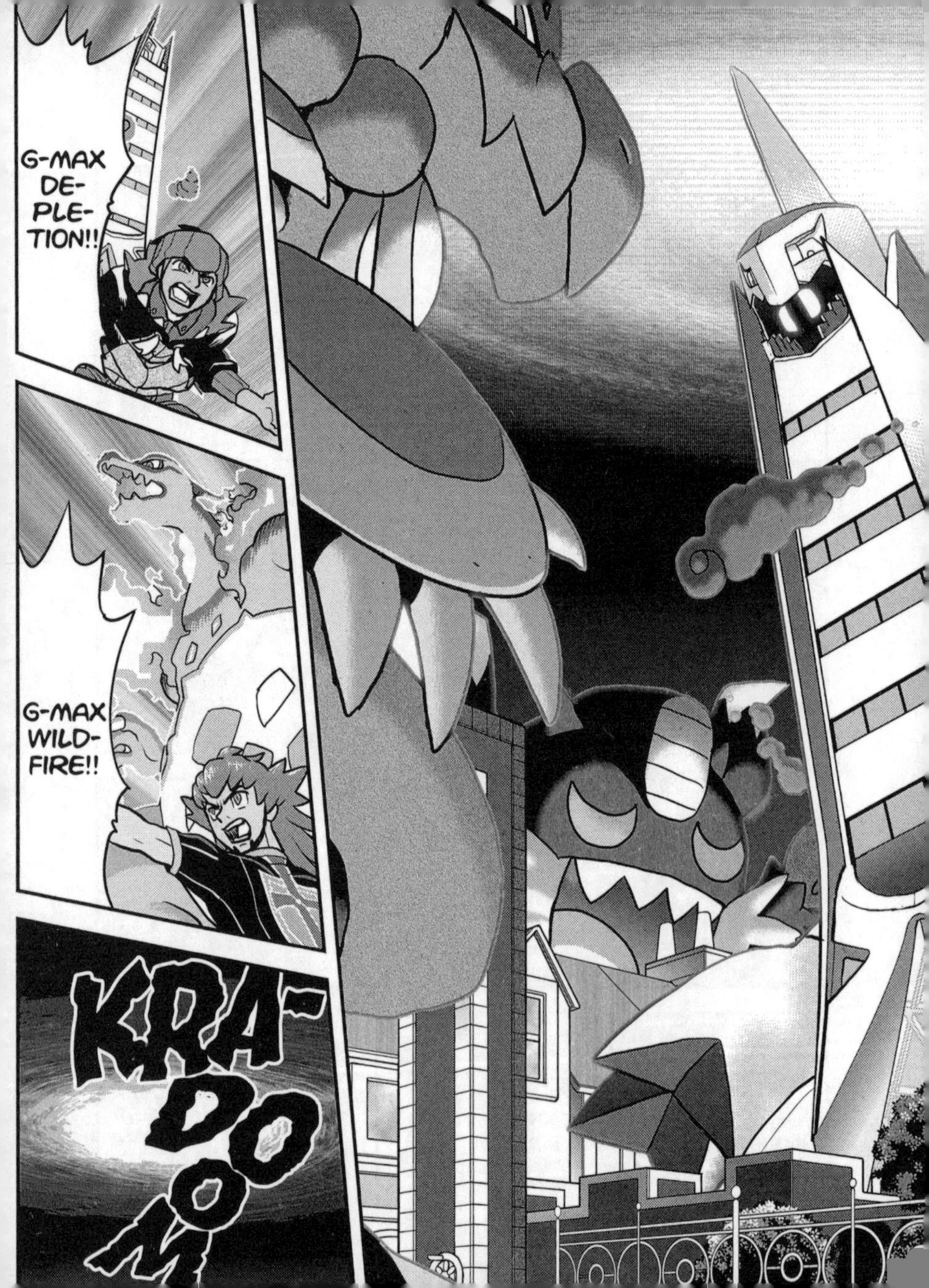
G-MAX DE-PLE-TION!!
G-MAX WILD-FIRE!!
KRA-DOOM

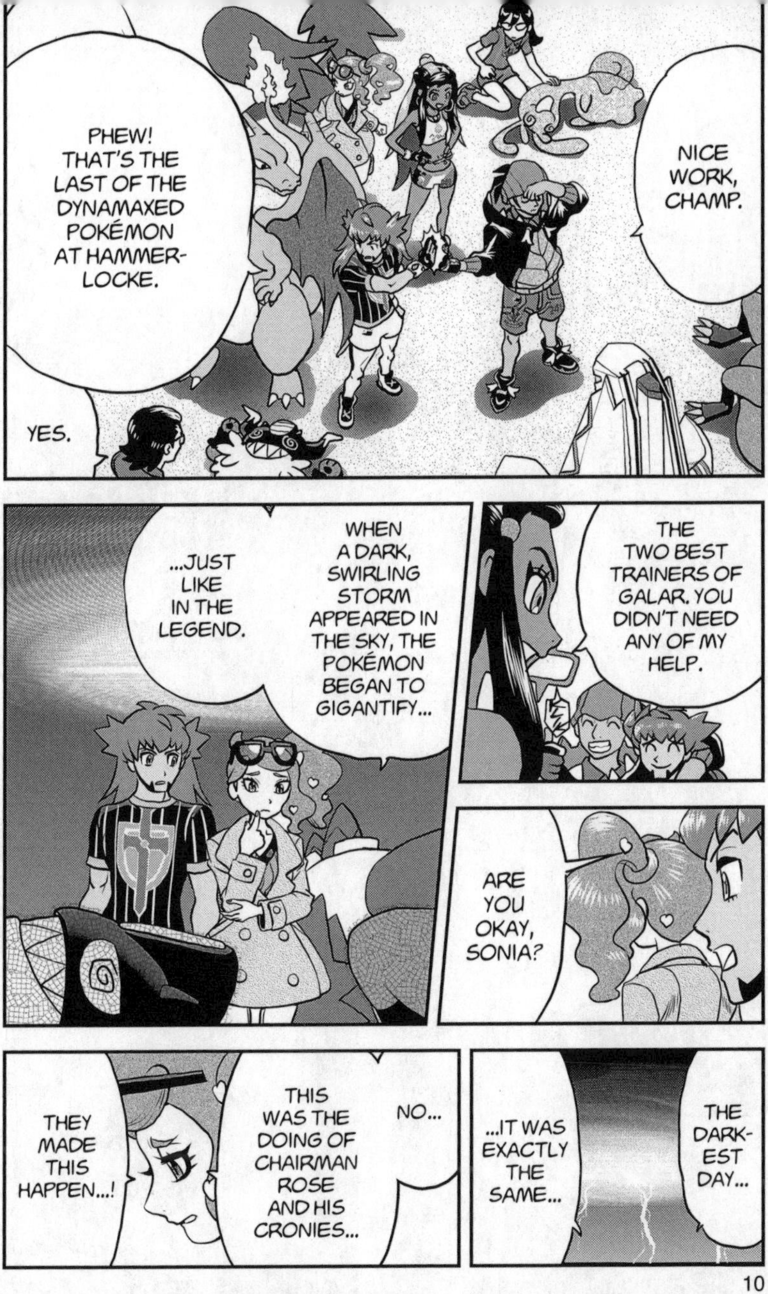
NICE WORK, CHAMP.
PHEW! THAT'S THE LAST OF THE DYNAMAXED POKÉMON AT HAMMER-LOCKE.
YES.
THE TWO BEST TRAINERS OF GALAR. YOU DIDN'T NEED ANY OF MY HELP.
ARE YOU OKAY, SONIA?
WHEN A DARK, SWIRLING STORM APPEARED IN THE SKY, THE POKÉMON BEGAN TO GIGANTIFY...
...JUST LIKE IN THE LEGEND.
THE DARK-EST DAY...
...IT WAS EXACTLY THE SAME...
NO...
THIS WAS THE DOING OF CHAIRMAN ROSE AND HIS CRONIES...
THEY MADE THIS HAPPEN...!

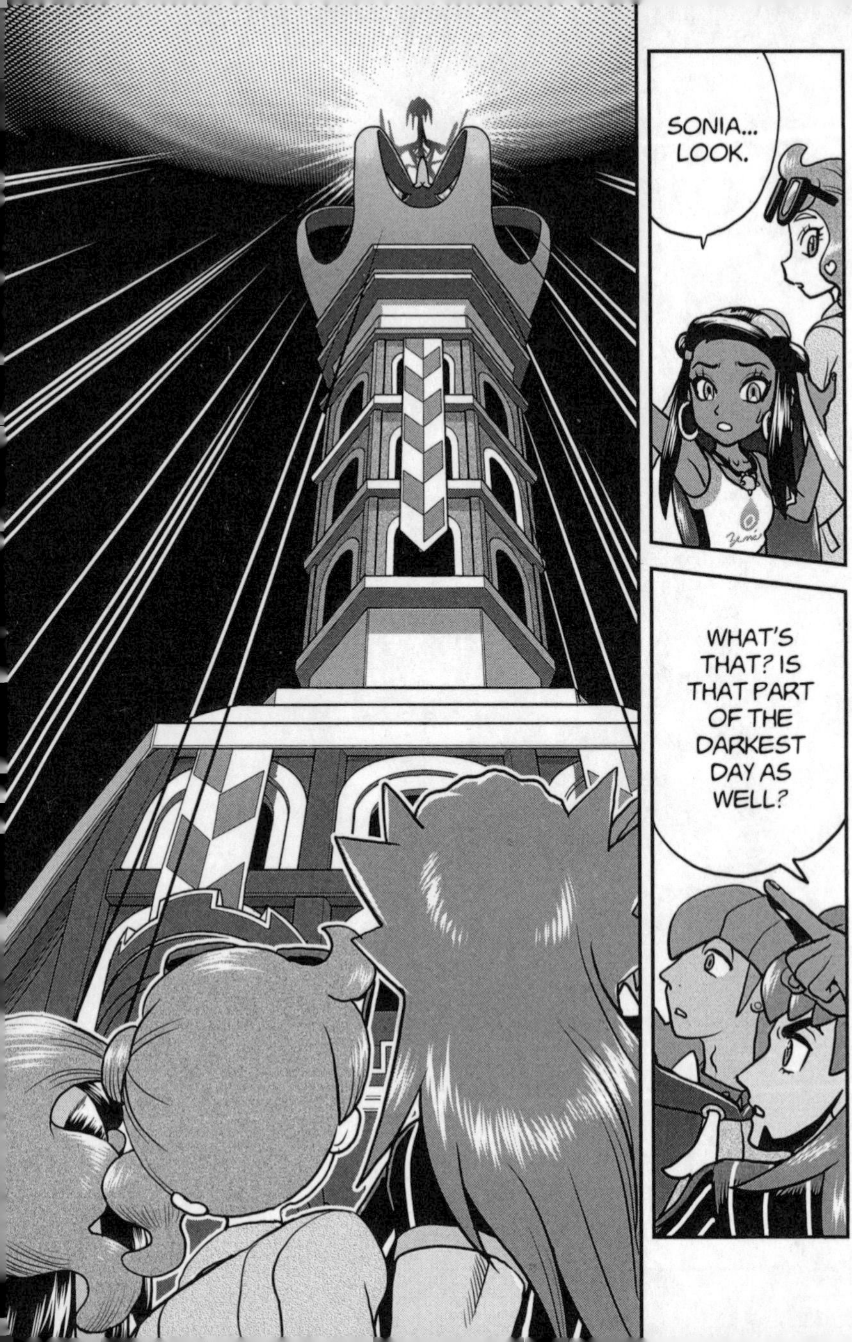
SONIA... LOOK.
WHAT'S THAT? IS THAT PART OF THE DARKEST DAY AS WELL?

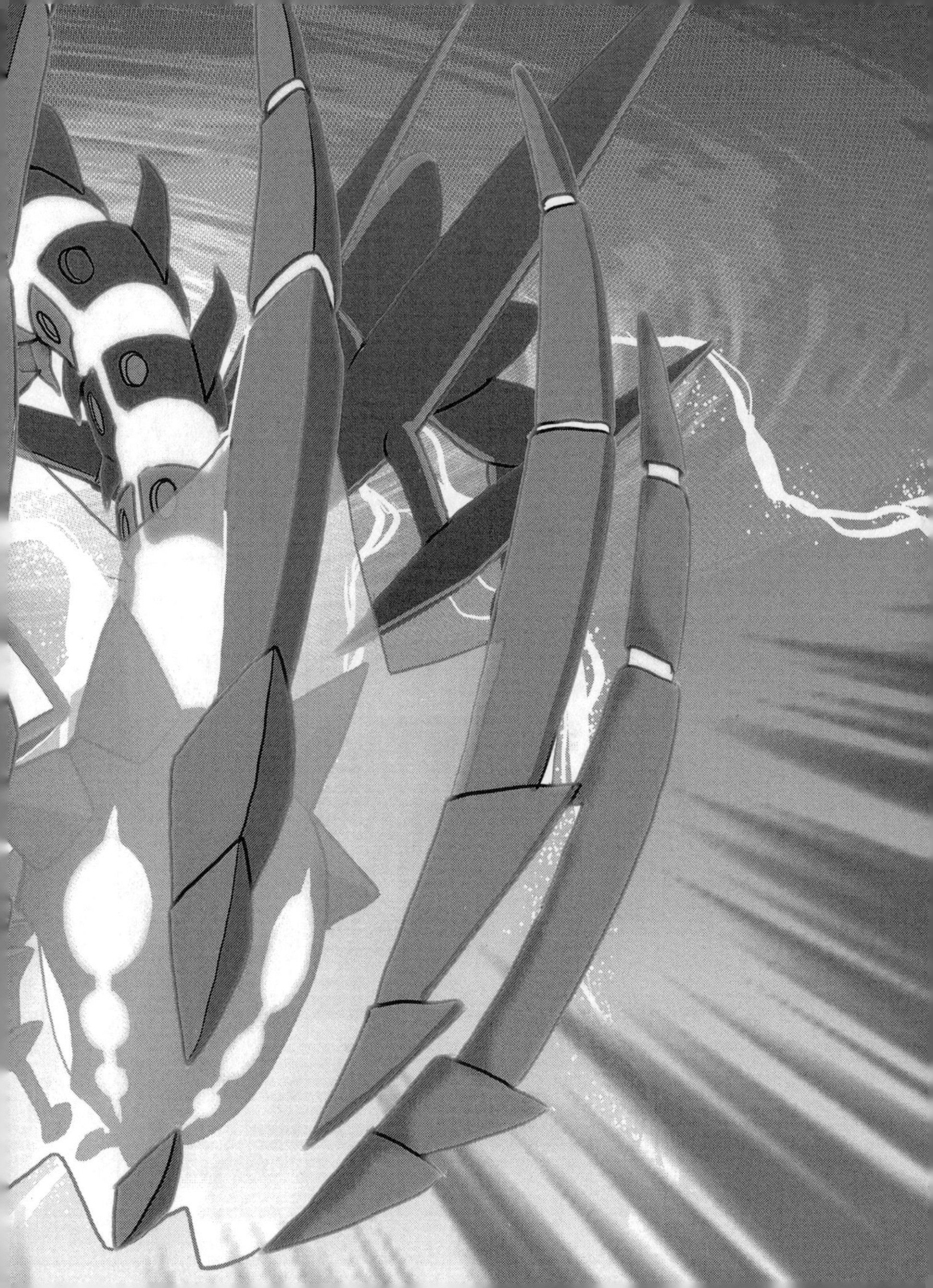

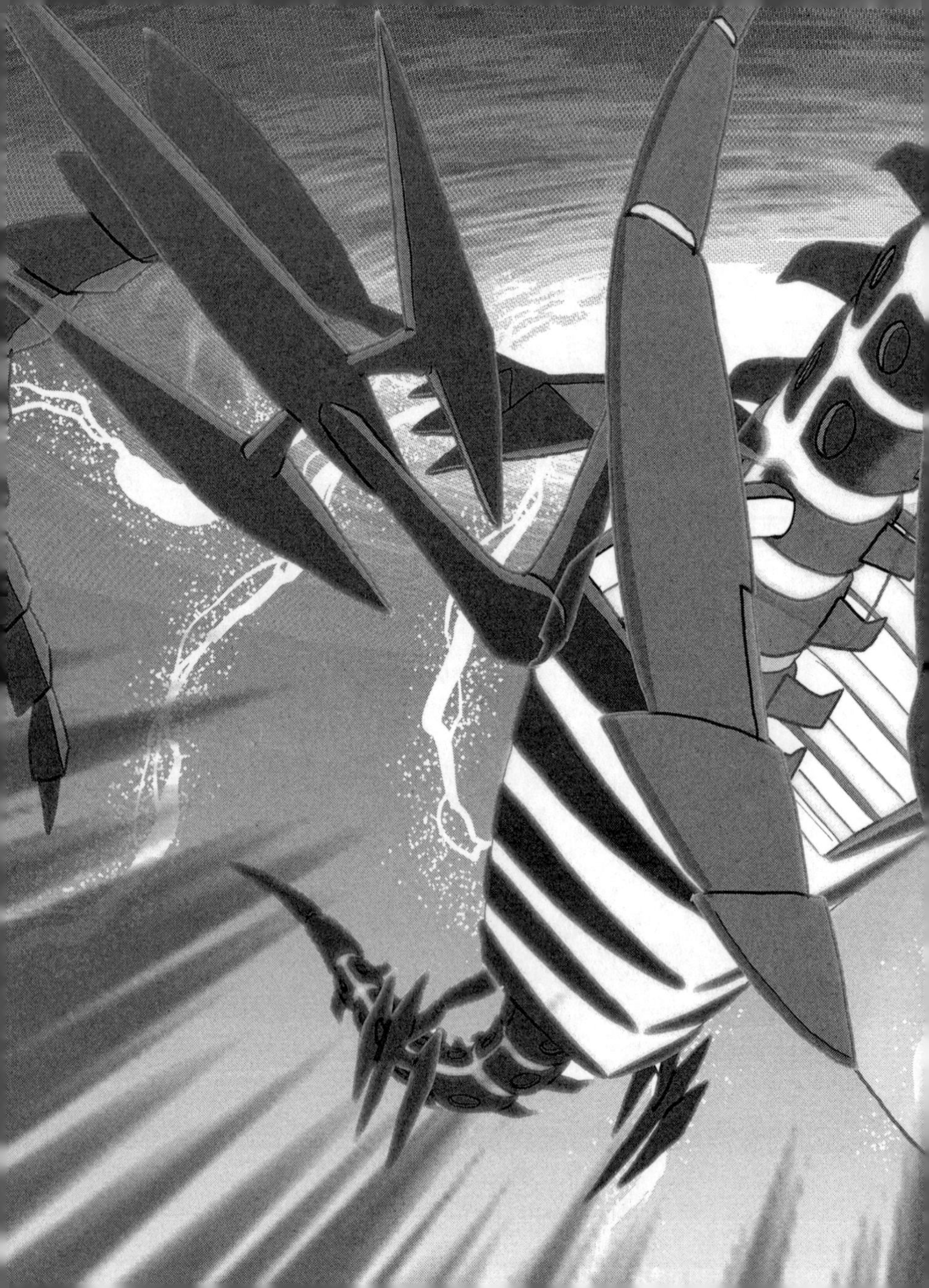

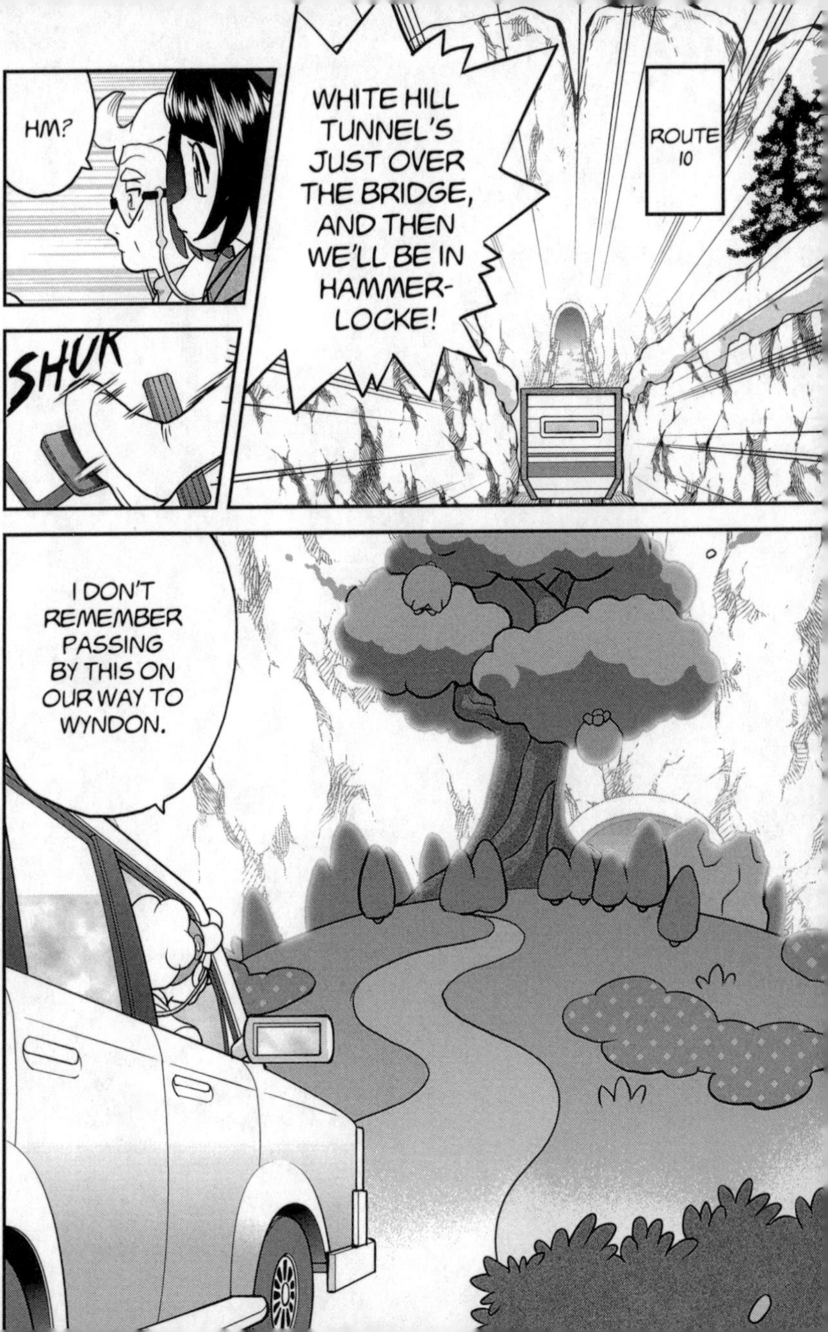
ROUTE 10
WHITE HILL TUNNEL'S JUST OVER THE BRIDGE, AND THEN WE'LL BE IN HAMMER-LOCKE!
HM?
SHUK
I DON'T REMEMBER PASSING BY THIS ON OUR WAY TO WYNDON.

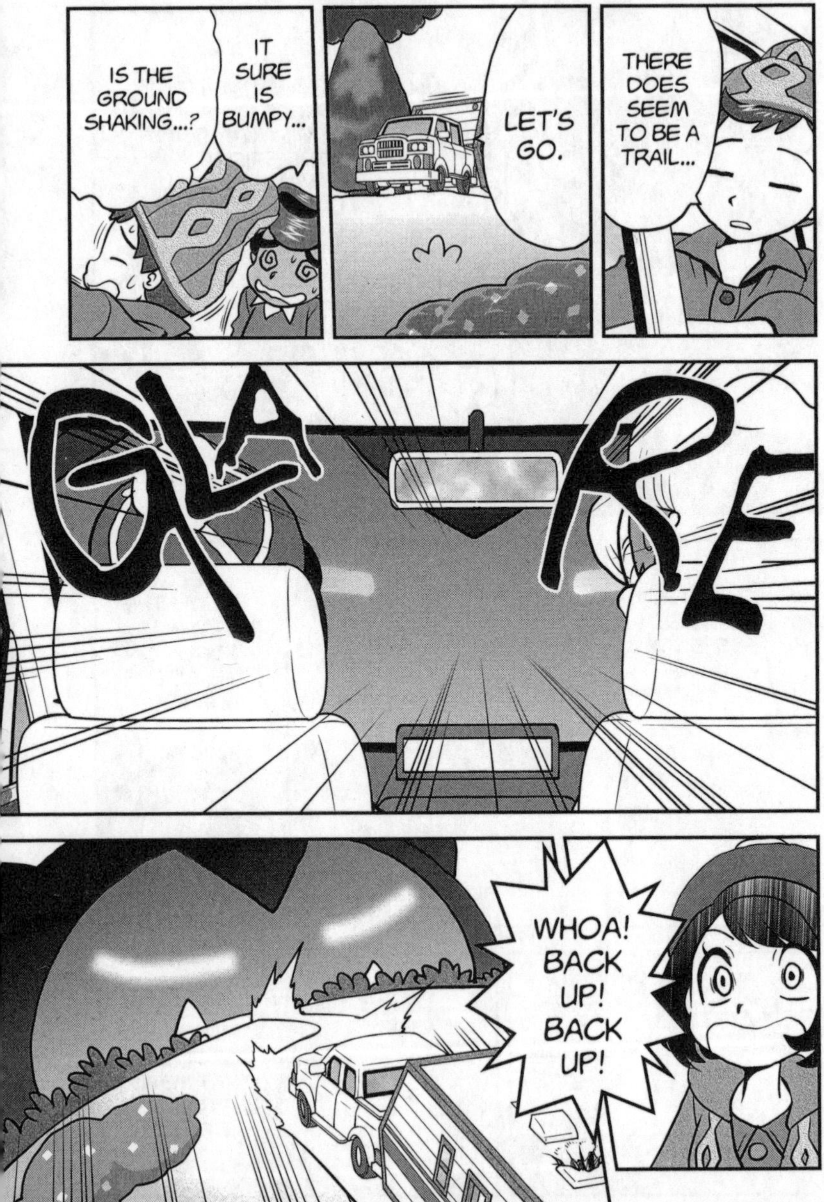
THERE DOES SEEM TO BE A TRAIL...
LET'S GO.
IT SURE IS BUMPY...
IS THE GROUND SHAKING...?
GLARE
WHOA! BACK UP! BACK UP!

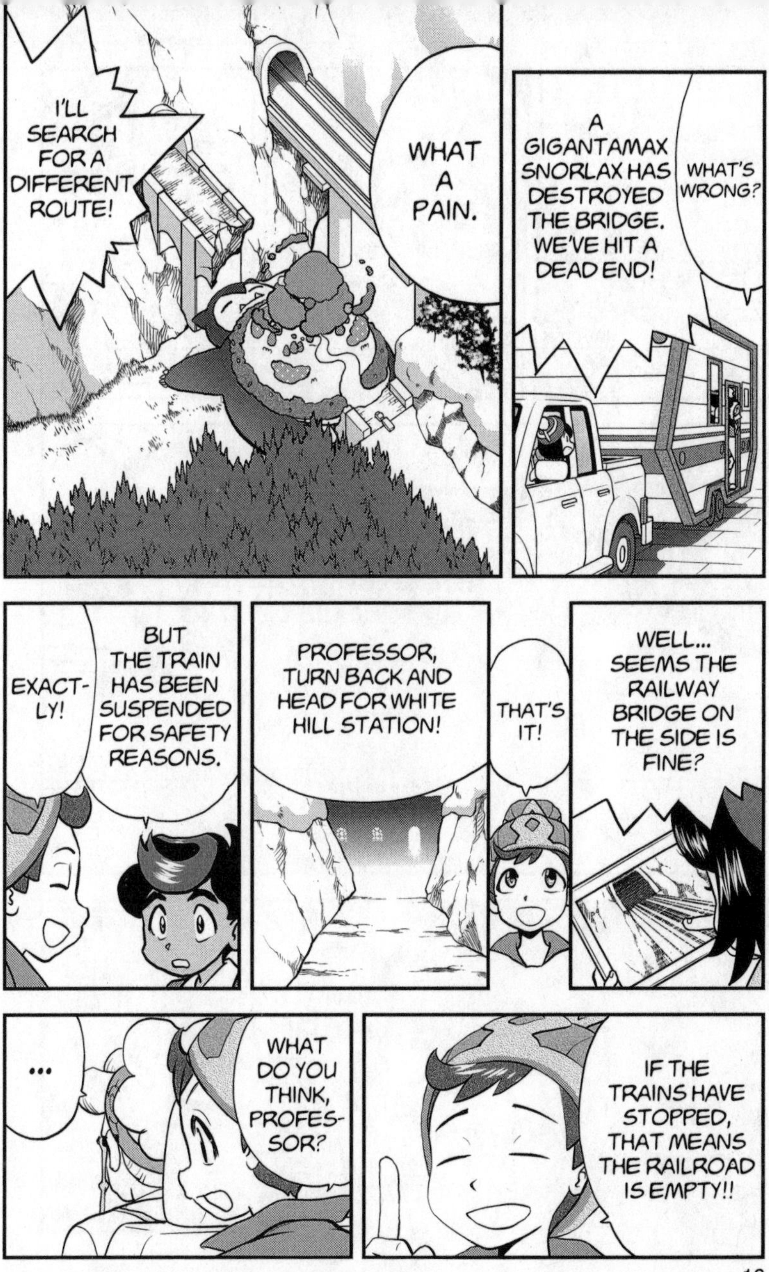
WHAT'S WRONG?
A GIGANTAMAX SNORLAX HAS DESTROYED THE BRIDGE. WE'VE HIT A DEAD END!
WHAT A PAIN.
I'LL SEARCH FOR A DIFFERENT ROUTE!
WELL... SEEMS THE RAILWAY BRIDGE ON THE SIDE IS FINE?
THAT'S IT!
PROFESSOR, TURN BACK AND HEAD FOR WHITE HILL STATION!
BUT THE TRAIN HAS BEEN SUSPENDED FOR SAFETY REASONS.
EXACT-LY!
IF THE TRAINS HAVE STOPPED, THAT MEANS THE RAILROAD IS EMPTY!!
WHAT DO YOU THINK, PROFES-SOR?
...

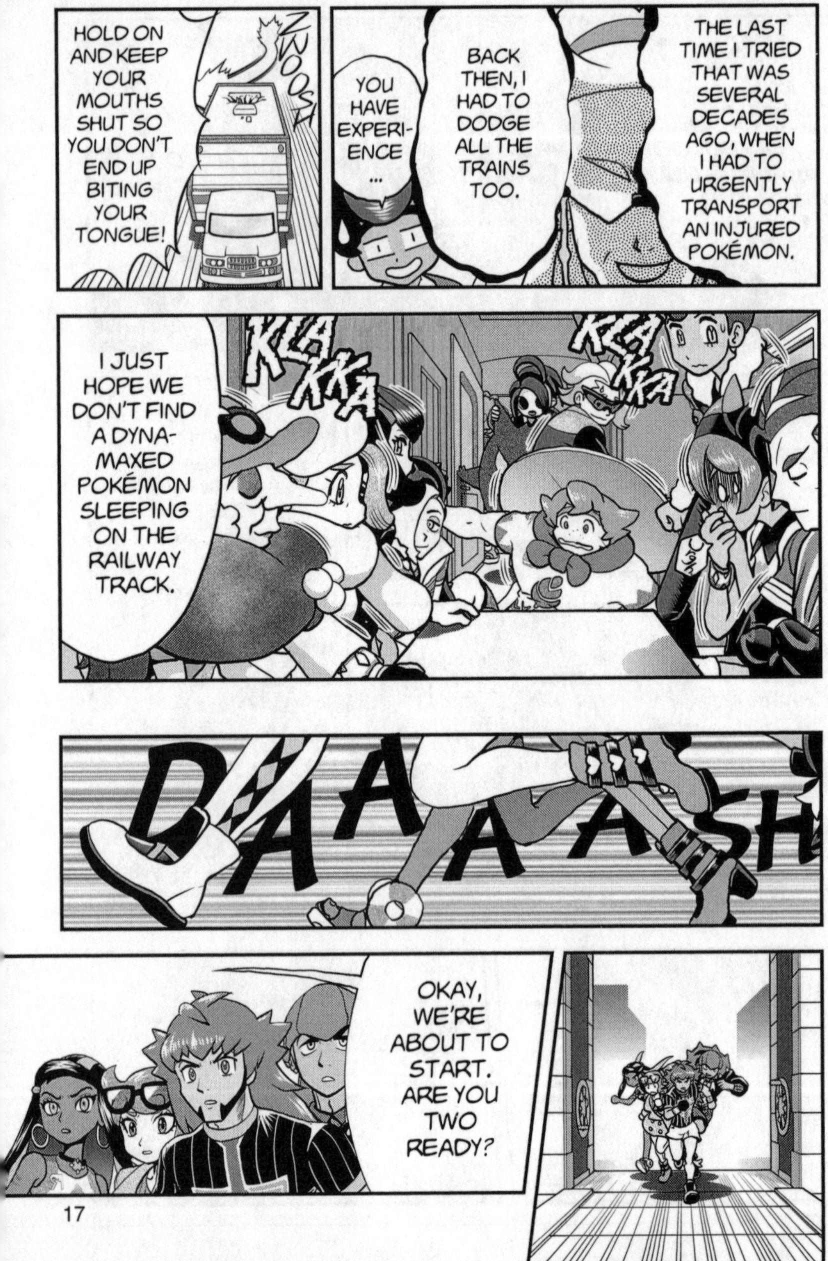
THE LAST TIME I TRIED THAT WAS SEVERAL DECADES AGO, WHEN I HAD TO URGENTLY TRANSPORT AN INJURED POKÉMON.
BACK THEN, I HAD TO DODGE ALL THE TRAINS TOO.
YOU HAVE EXPERIENCE ...
ZWOOSH
HOLD ON AND KEEP YOUR MOUTHS SHUT SO YOU DON'T END UP BITING YOUR TONGUE!
KLAKKA
KLAKKA
I JUST HOPE WE DON'T FIND A DYNAMAXED POKÉMON SLEEPING ON THE RAILWAY TRACK.
DAAAASH
OKAY, WE'RE ABOUT TO START. ARE YOU TWO READY?

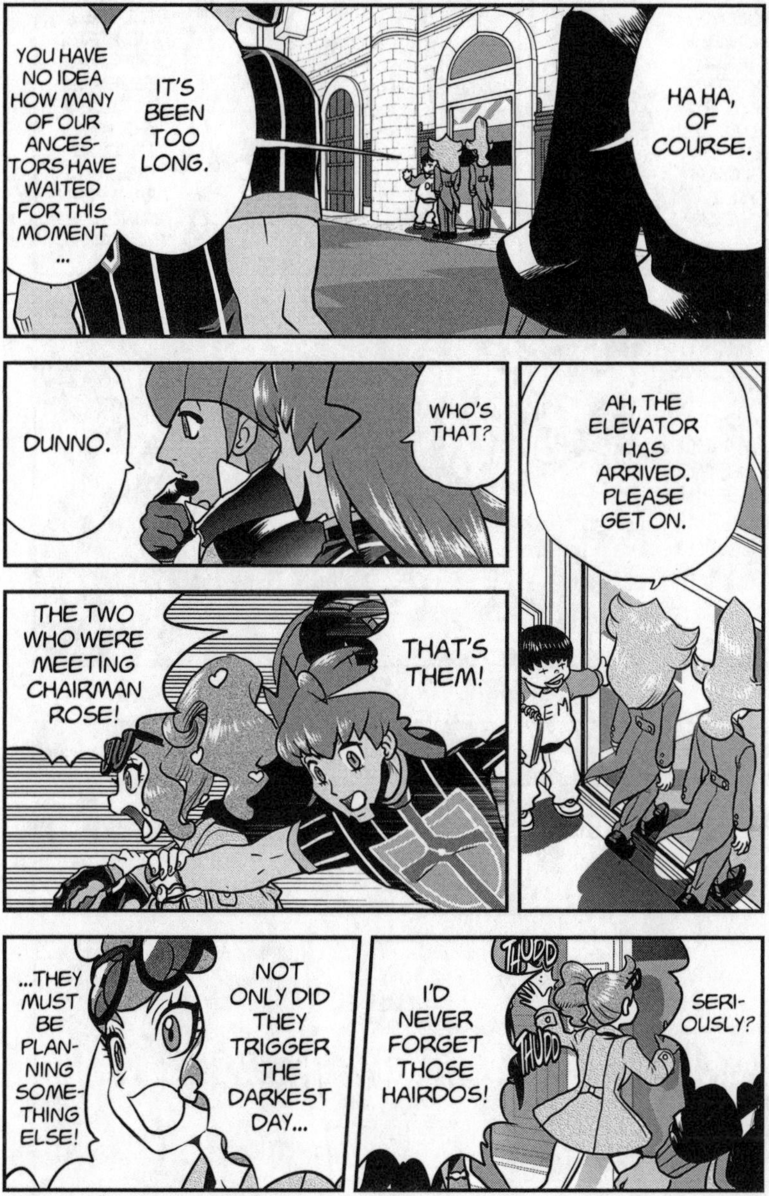
HA HA, OF COURSE.
IT'S BEEN TOO LONG.
YOU HAVE NO IDEA HOW MANY OF OUR ANCESTORS HAVE WAITED FOR THIS MOMENT ...
AH, THE ELEVATOR HAS ARRIVED. PLEASE GET ON.
WHO'S THAT?
DUNNO.
THAT'S THEM!
THE TWO WHO WERE MEETING CHAIRMAN ROSE!
SERIOUSLY?
THUDD
THUDD
I'D NEVER FORGET THOSE HAIRDOS!
NOT ONLY DID THEY TRIGGER THE DARKEST DAY...
...THEY MUST BE PLANNING SOMETHING ELSE!

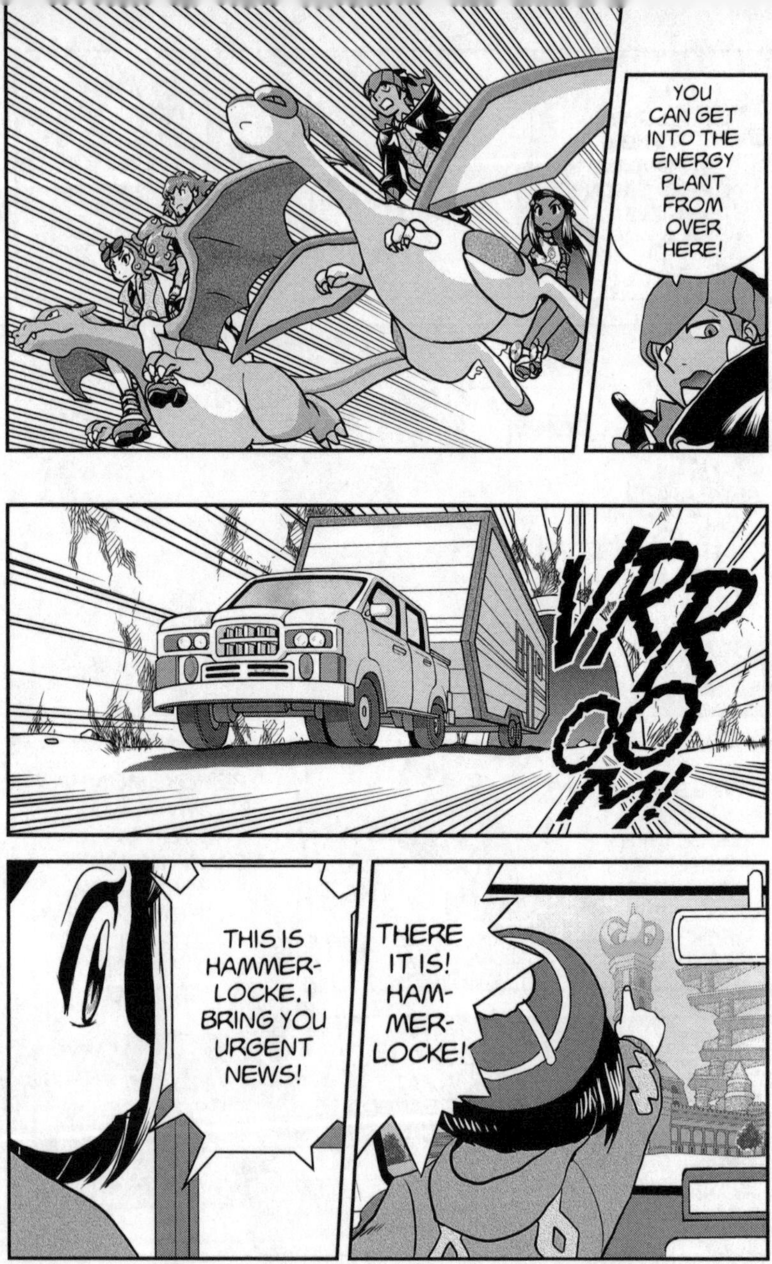
YOU CAN GET INTO THE ENERGY PLANT FROM OVER HERE!
VRROOOM!
THERE IT IS! HAMMERLOCKE!
THIS IS HAMMERLOCKE. I BRING YOU URGENT NEWS!

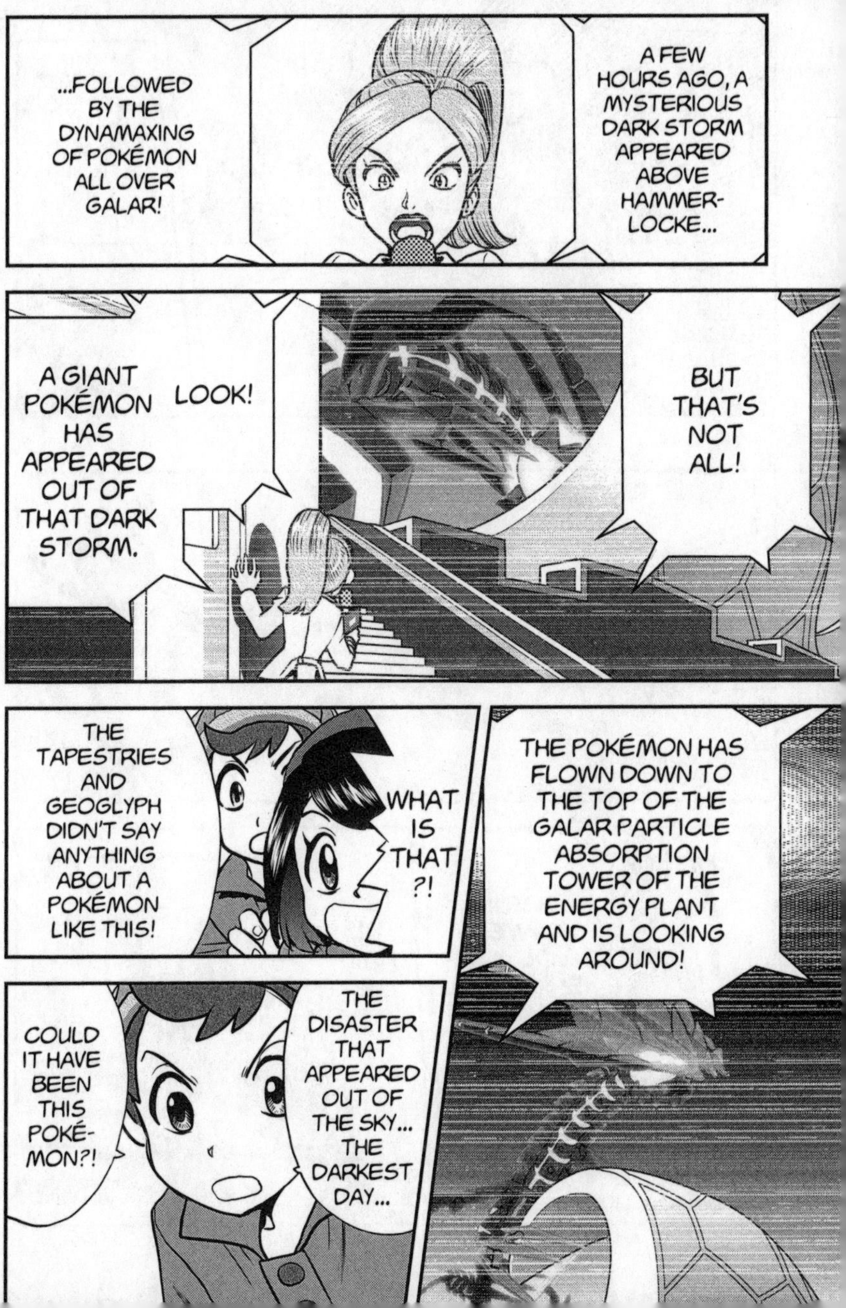
A FEW HOURS AGO, A MYSTERIOUS DARK STORM APPEARED ABOVE HAMMER-LOCKE...
...FOLLOWED BY THE DYNAMAXING OF POKÉMON ALL OVER GALAR!
BUT THAT'S NOT ALL!
LOOK!
A GIANT POKÉMON HAS APPEARED OUT OF THAT DARK STORM.
THE POKÉMON HAS FLOWN DOWN TO THE TOP OF THE GALAR PARTICLE ABSORPTION TOWER OF THE ENERGY PLANT AND IS LOOKING AROUND!
WHAT IS THAT?!
THE TAPESTRIES AND GEOGLYPH DIDN'T SAY ANYTHING ABOUT A POKÉMON LIKE THIS!
THE DISASTER THAT APPEARED OUT OF THE SKY... THE DARKEST DAY...
COULD IT HAVE BEEN THIS POKÉ-MON?!

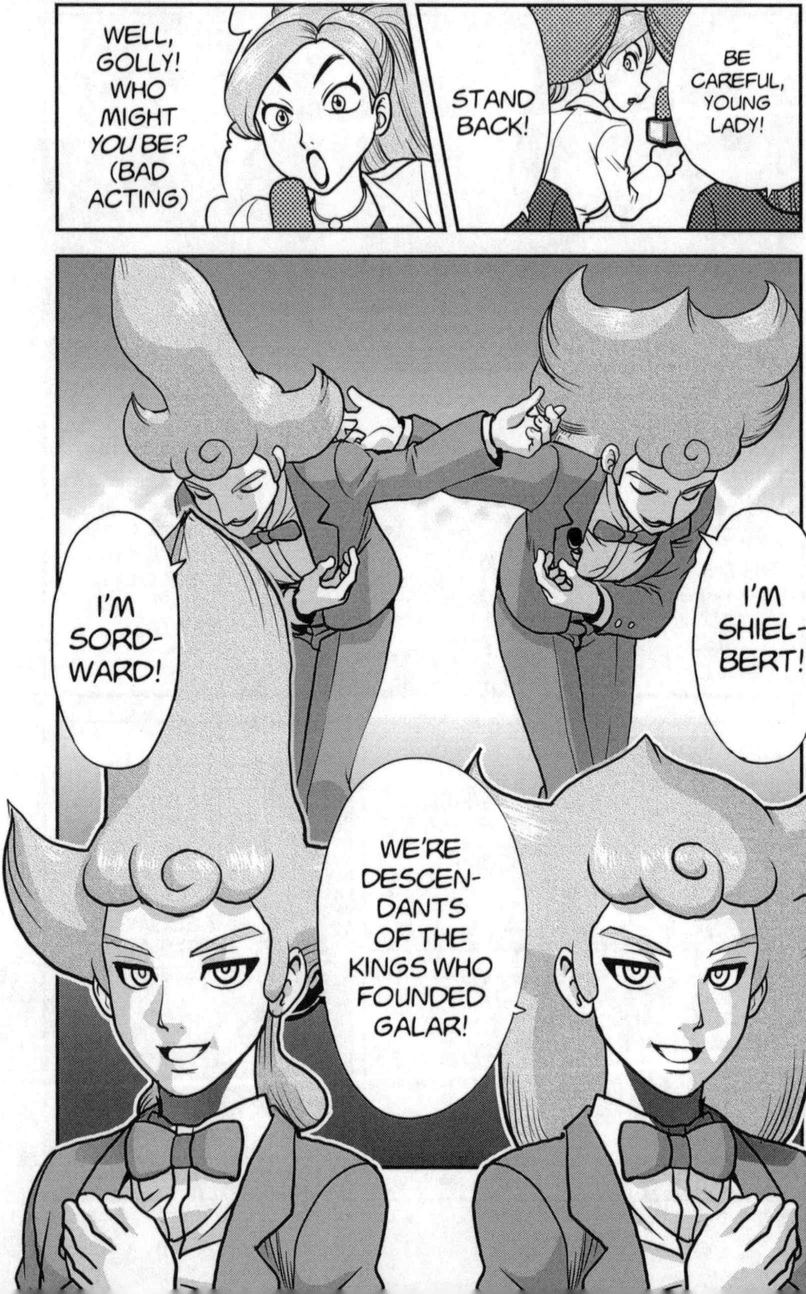
BE CAREFUL, YOUNG LADY!
STAND BACK!
WELL, GOLLY! WHO MIGHT *YOU* BE? (BAD ACTING)
I'M SHIEL-BERT!
I'M SORD-WARD!
WE'RE DESCEN-DANTS OF THE KINGS WHO FOUNDED GALAR!

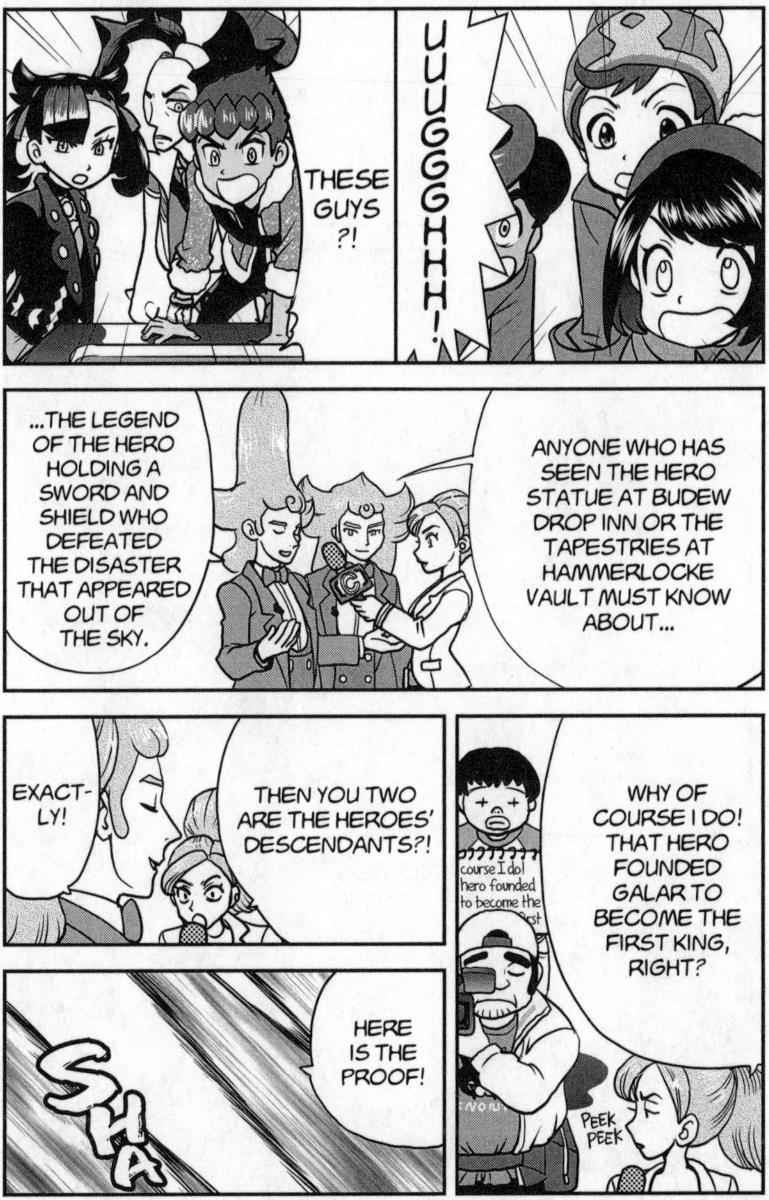
UUUGGGHHH!
THESE GUYS ?!
ANYONE WHO HAS SEEN THE HERO STATUE AT BUDEW DROP INN OR THE TAPESTRIES AT HAMMERLOCKE VAULT MUST KNOW ABOUT...
...THE LEGEND OF THE HERO HOLDING A SWORD AND SHIELD WHO DEFEATED THE DISASTER THAT APPEARED OUT OF THE SKY.
WHY OF COURSE I DO! THAT HERO FOUNDED GALAR TO BECOME THE FIRST KING, RIGHT?
course I do!
hero founded
to become the
PEEK PEEK
THEN YOU TWO ARE THE HEROES' DESCENDANTS?!
EXACT-LY!
HERE IS THE PROOF!
SHA

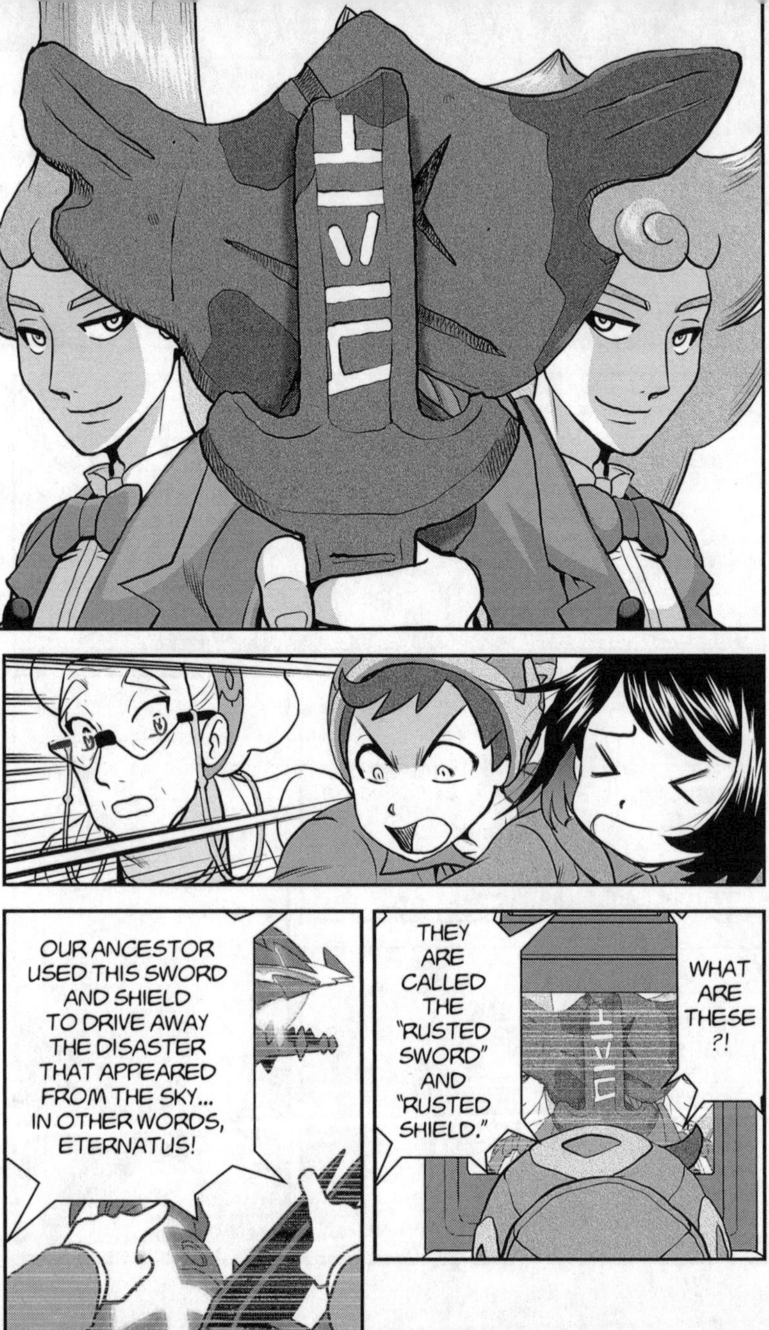
WHAT ARE THESE?!
THEY ARE CALLED THE "RUSTED SWORD" AND "RUSTED SHIELD."
OUR ANCESTOR USED THIS SWORD AND SHIELD TO DRIVE AWAY THE DISASTER THAT APPEARED FROM THE SKY... IN OTHER WORDS, ETERNATUS!

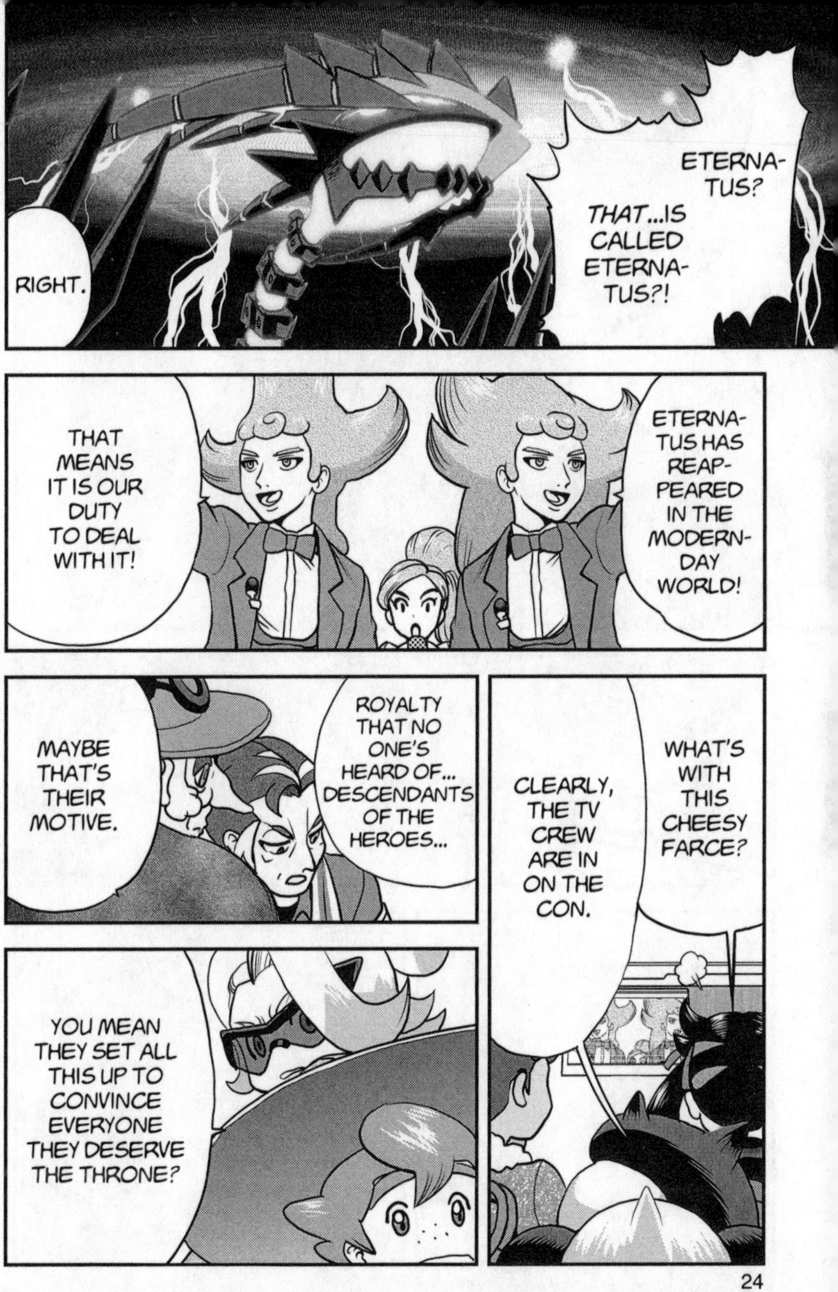
ETERNATUS?
THAT...IS CALLED ETERNATUS?!
RIGHT.
ETERNATUS HAS REAPPEARED IN THE MODERN-DAY WORLD!
THAT MEANS IT IS OUR DUTY TO DEAL WITH IT!
WHAT'S WITH THIS CHEESY FARCE?
CLEARLY, THE TV CREW ARE IN ON THE CON.
ROYALTY THAT NO ONE'S HEARD OF... DESCENDANTS OF THE HEROES...
MAYBE THAT'S THEIR MOTIVE.
YOU MEAN THEY SET ALL THIS UP TO CONVINCE EVERYONE THEY DESERVE THE THRONE?

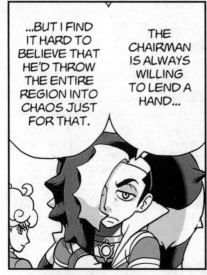

THEN WHY DID THEY WAIT UNTIL NOW?
AND WHY DID CHAIRMAN ROSE HELP THEM?
THE CHAIRMAN IS ALWAYS WILLING TO LEND A HAND...
...BUT I FIND IT HARD TO BELIEVE THAT HE'D THROW THE ENTIRE REGION INTO CHAOS JUST FOR THAT.
RRING
RRING
HELLO?
YES... YES...
OKAY.
WHAT'S THE MATTER?
THERE ARE SO MANY DYNAMAXED POKÉMON AT MOTOSTOKE THERE AREN'T ENOUGH TRAINERS AT MY GYM TO DEAL WITH THEM!
HMM. IT MAY BE A GOOD IDEA FOR ALL OF US TO RETURN TO OUR TOWNS FOR NOW.
EVERYONE WILL FEEL SAFER JUST TO SEE A GYM LEADER AROUND.

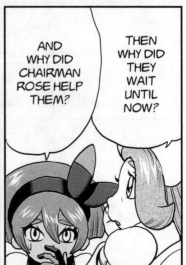

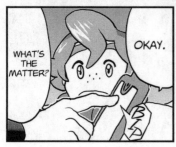

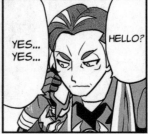

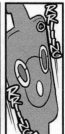

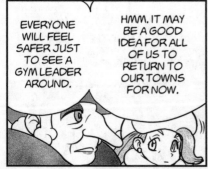

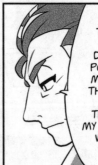

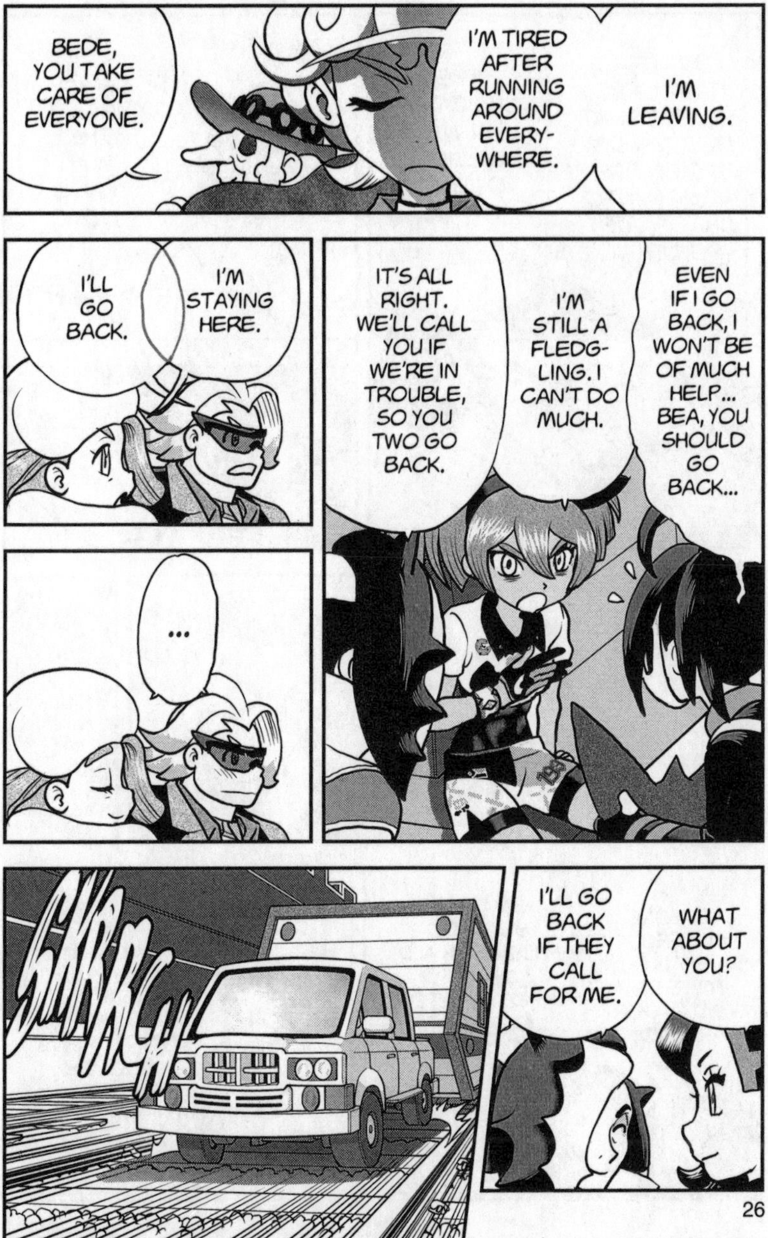
I'M LEAVING.
I'M TIRED AFTER RUNNING AROUND EVERY-WHERE.
BEDE, YOU TAKE CARE OF EVERYONE.
EVEN IF I GO BACK, I WON'T BE OF MUCH HELP... BEA, YOU SHOULD GO BACK...
I'M STILL A FLEDG-LING. I CAN'T DO MUCH.
IT'S ALL RIGHT. WE'LL CALL YOU IF WE'RE IN TROUBLE, SO YOU TWO GO BACK.
I'M STAYING HERE.
I'LL GO BACK.
...
WHAT ABOUT YOU?
I'LL GO BACK IF THEY CALL FOR ME.
SKRRCH

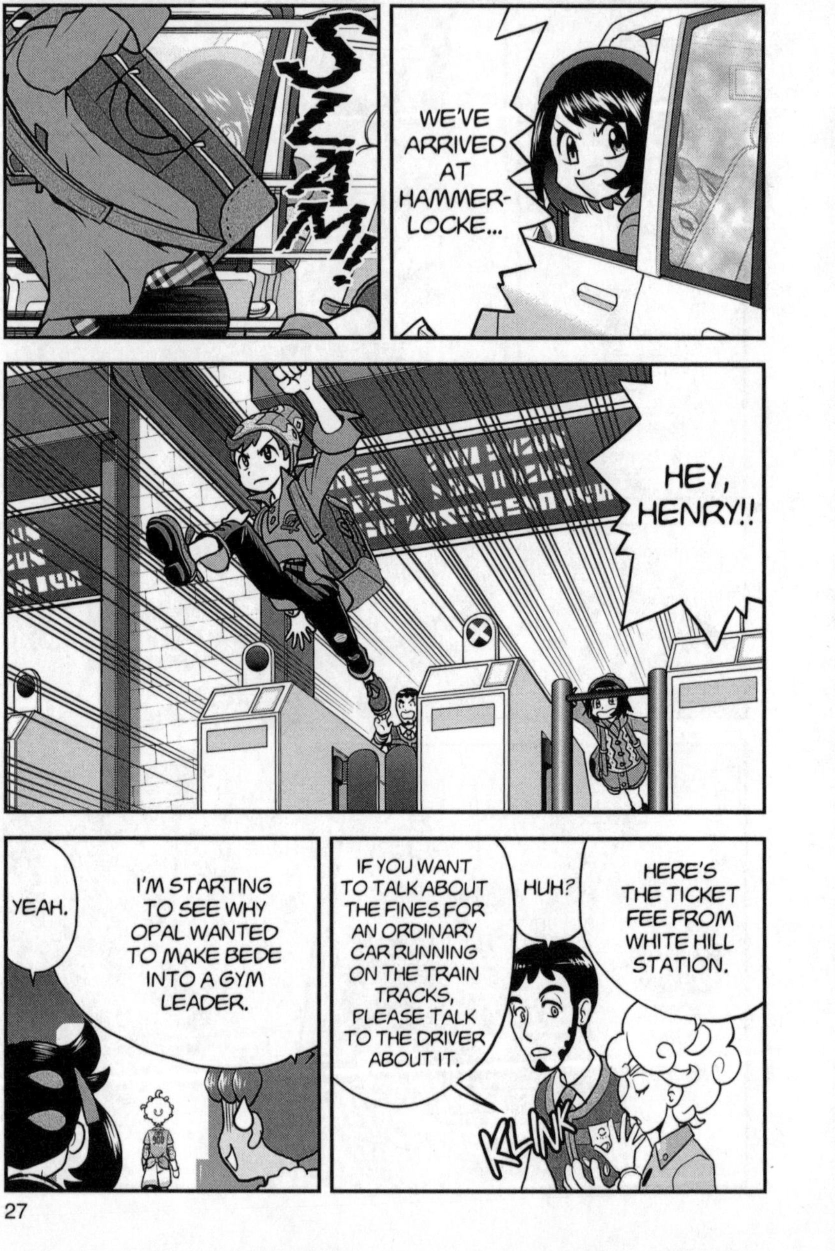
WE'VE ARRIVED AT HAMMER-LOCKE...
SLAM!!
HEY, HENRY!!
HERE'S THE TICKET FEE FROM WHITE HILL STATION.
HUH?
IF YOU WANT TO TALK ABOUT THE FINES FOR AN ORDINARY CAR RUNNING ON THE TRAIN TRACKS, PLEASE TALK TO THE DRIVER ABOUT IT.
KLINK
I'M STARTING TO SEE WHY OPAL WANTED TO MAKE BEDE INTO A GYM LEADER.
YEAH.

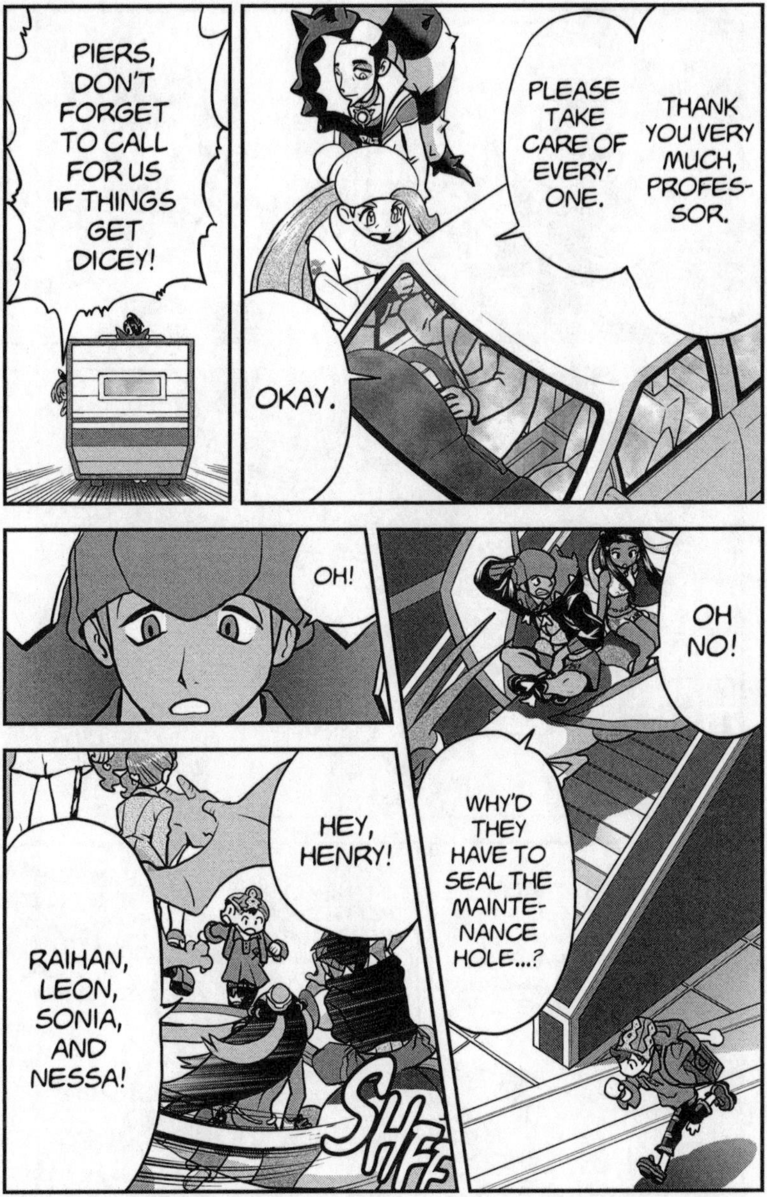
THANK YOU VERY MUCH, PROFESSOR.
PLEASE TAKE CARE OF EVERYONE.
OKAY.
PIERS, DON'T FORGET TO CALL FOR US IF THINGS GET DICEY!
OH NO!
WHY'D THEY HAVE TO SEAL THE MAINTENANCE HOLE...?
OH!
HEY, HENRY!
RAIHAN, LEON, SONIA, AND NESSA!
SHFF

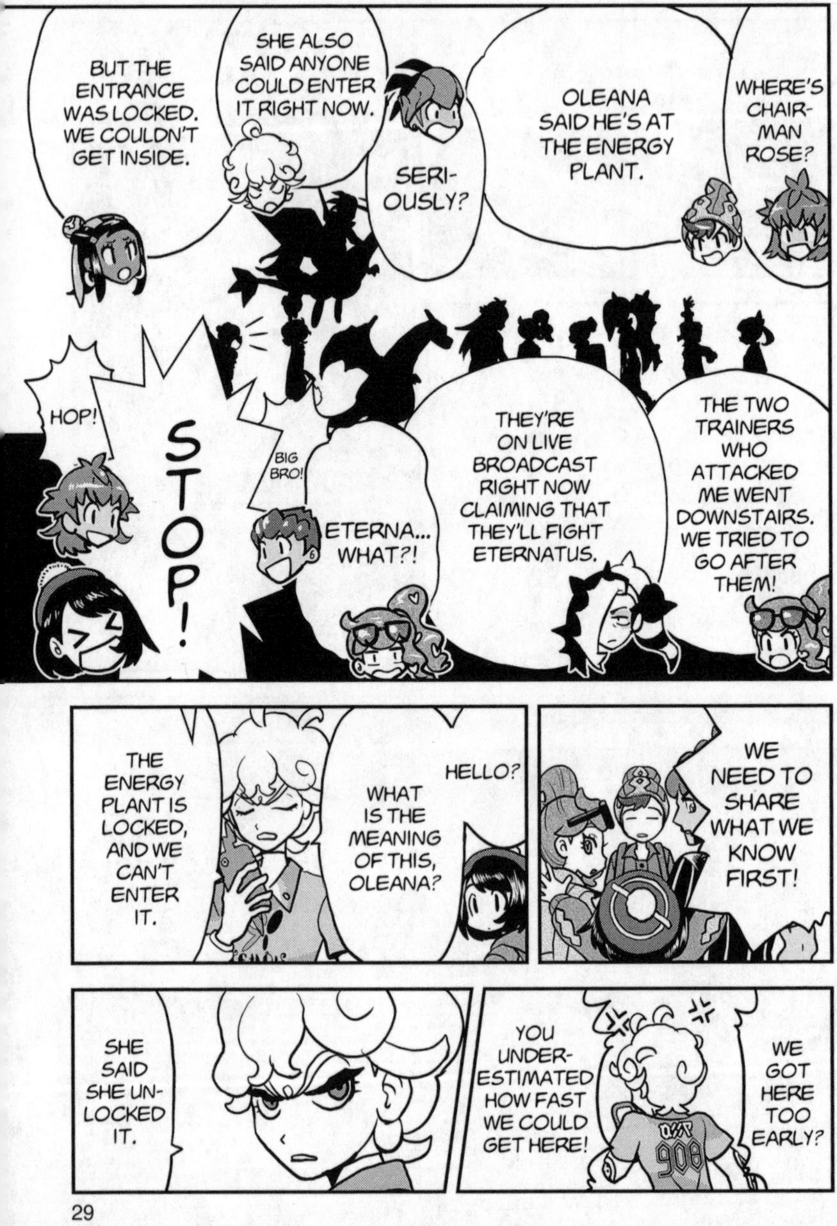
WHERE'S CHAIRMAN ROSE?
OLEANA SAID HE'S AT THE ENERGY PLANT.
SERIOUSLY?
SHE ALSO SAID ANYONE COULD ENTER IT RIGHT NOW.
BUT THE ENTRANCE WAS LOCKED. WE COULDN'T GET INSIDE.
THE TWO TRAINERS WHO ATTACKED ME WENT DOWNSTAIRS. WE TRIED TO GO AFTER THEM!
THEY'RE ON LIVE BROADCAST RIGHT NOW CLAIMING THAT THEY'LL FIGHT ETERNATUS.
ETERNA... WHAT?!
BIG BRO!
STOP!
HOP!
WE NEED TO SHARE WHAT WE KNOW FIRST!
HELLO?
WHAT IS THE MEANING OF THIS, OLEANA?
THE ENERGY PLANT IS LOCKED, AND WE CAN'T ENTER IT.
WE GOT HERE TOO EARLY?
YOU UNDERESTIMATED HOW FAST WE COULD GET HERE!
SHE SAID SHE UNLOCKED IT.

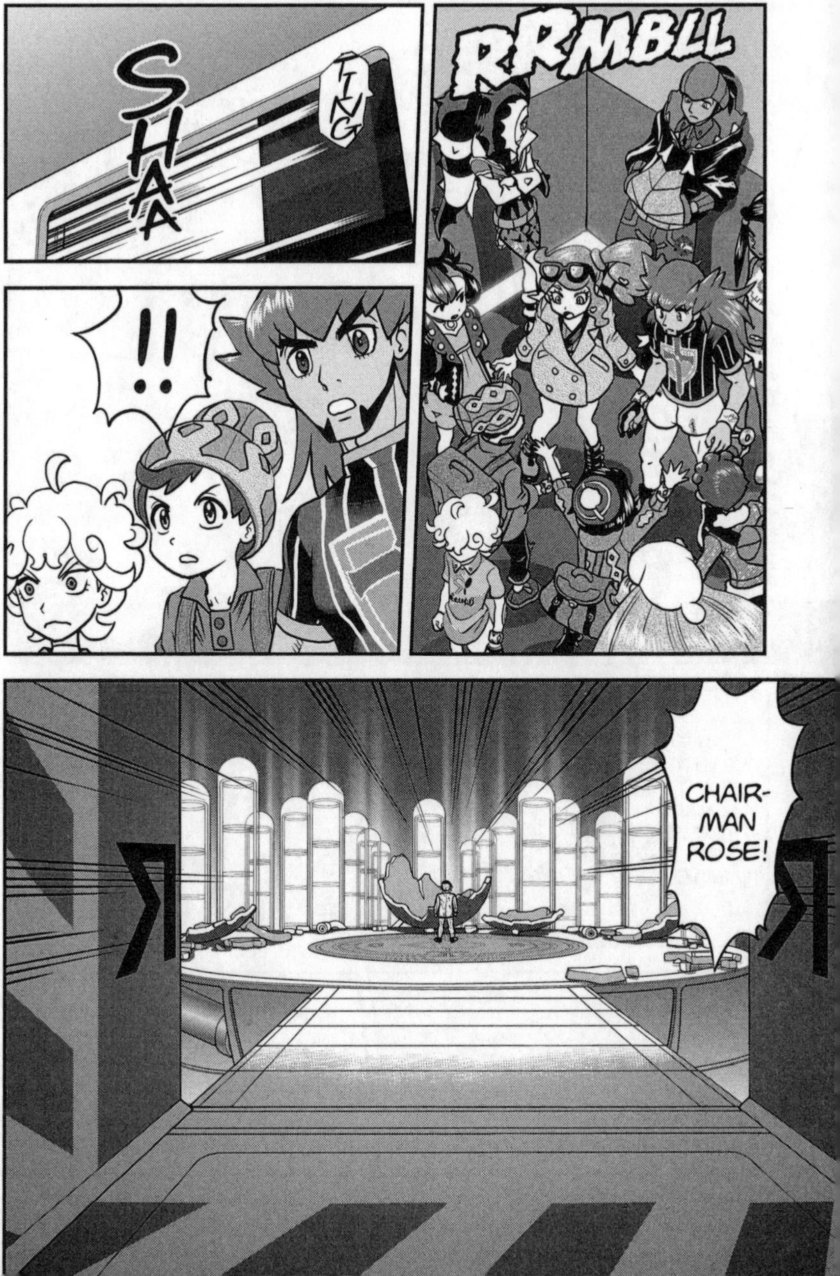
RRMBLL
SHAA
TING
!!
CHAIR-
MAN
ROSE!

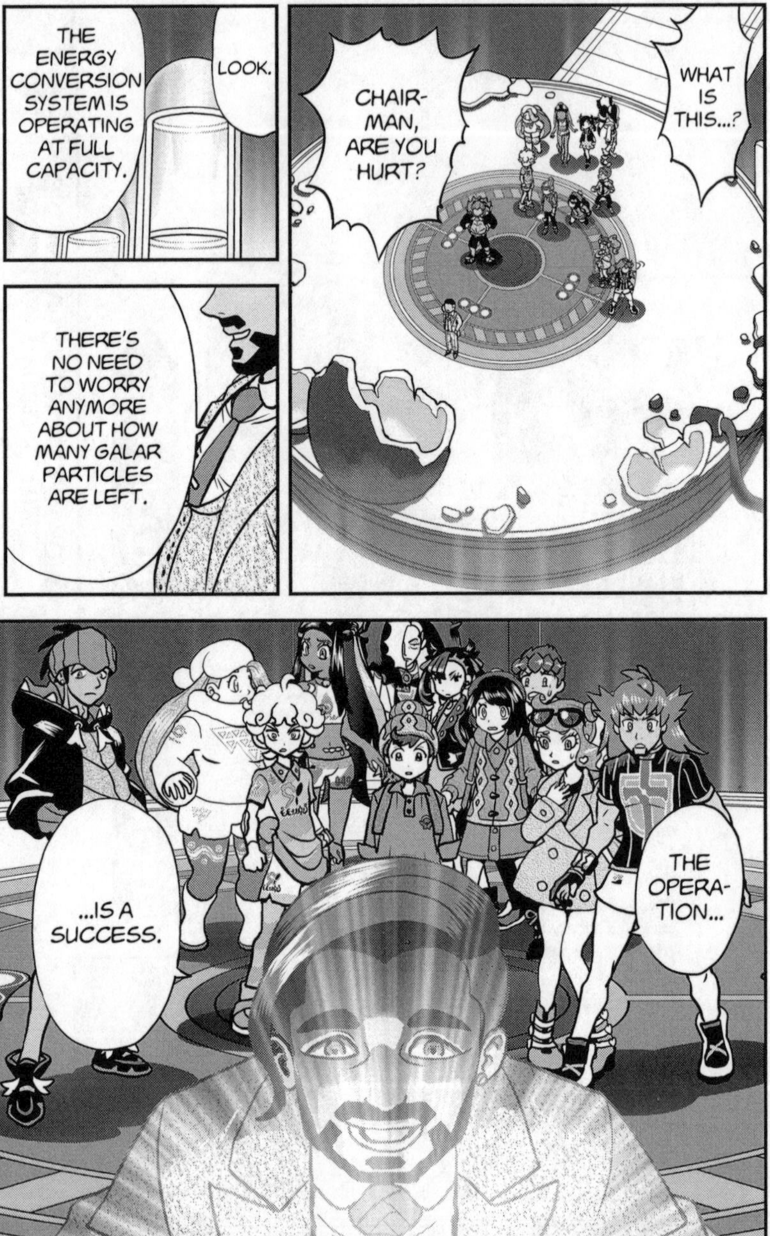
WHAT IS THIS...?
CHAIR-MAN, ARE YOU HURT?
LOOK.
THE ENERGY CONVERSION SYSTEM IS OPERATING AT FULL CAPACITY.
THERE'S NO NEED TO WORRY ANYMORE ABOUT HOW MANY GALAR PARTICLES ARE LEFT.
THE OPERA-TION...
...IS A SUCCESS.

GIGANTAMAX CENTISKORCH

TYPE	Fire, Bug
ABILITY	Flash Fire White Smoke
G-MAX MOVE	G-Max Centiferno

HEIGHT	246'01"+
WEIGHT	??? lbs

ORDINARY
CENTISKORCH

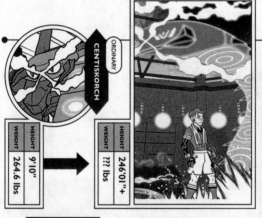

HEIGHT	9'10"
WEIGHT	264.6 lbs

Gigantamaxing makes its body grow larger and longer. Its body temperature rises dramatically to over a horrifying 1,800 degrees Fahrenheit, creating heatwaves!!

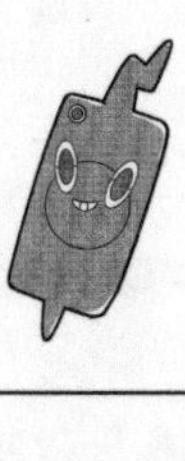

STRATEGY NOTES

Its special Fire-type move while Gigantamaxed is G-Max Centiferno. It traps the opponent inside fire, so you need to be careful. Once you are trapped, you will be unable to swap your Pokémon, so be ready to bear the attack. You will need to have good defense, but once you survive the attack, victory will be only a step away!!

Adventure 27 Shock!! Chairman Rose's Plan

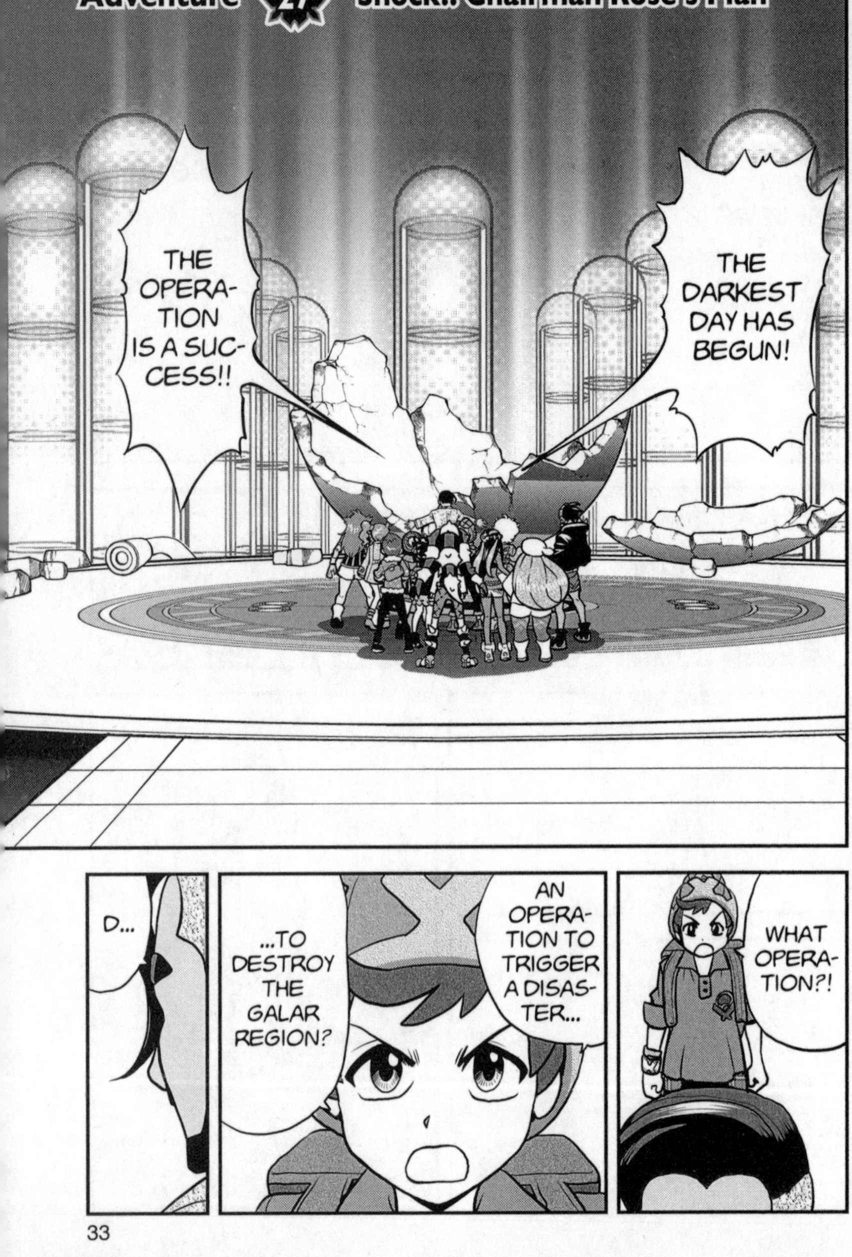
THE DARKEST DAY HAS BEGUN!
THE OPERATION IS A SUCCESS!!
WHAT OPERATION?!
AN OPERATION TO TRIGGER A DISASTER...
...TO DESTROY THE GALAR REGION?
D...

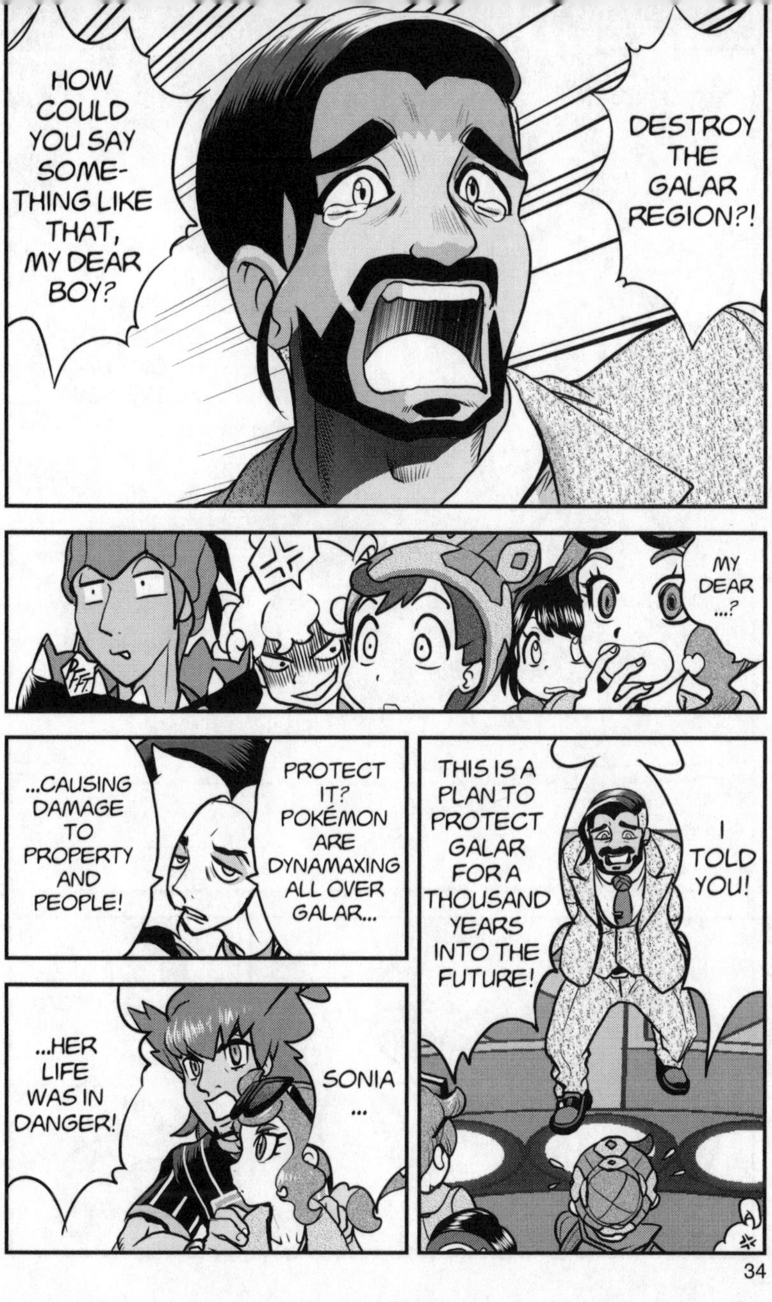
DESTROY THE GALAR REGION?!
HOW COULD YOU SAY SOME-THING LIKE THAT, MY DEAR BOY?
MY DEAR ...?
PFFT.
I TOLD YOU!
THIS IS A PLAN TO PROTECT GALAR FOR A THOUSAND YEARS INTO THE FUTURE!
PROTECT IT? POKÉMON ARE DYNAMAXING ALL OVER GALAR...
...CAUSING DAMAGE TO PROPERTY AND PEOPLE!
SONIA ...
...HER LIFE WAS IN DANGER!

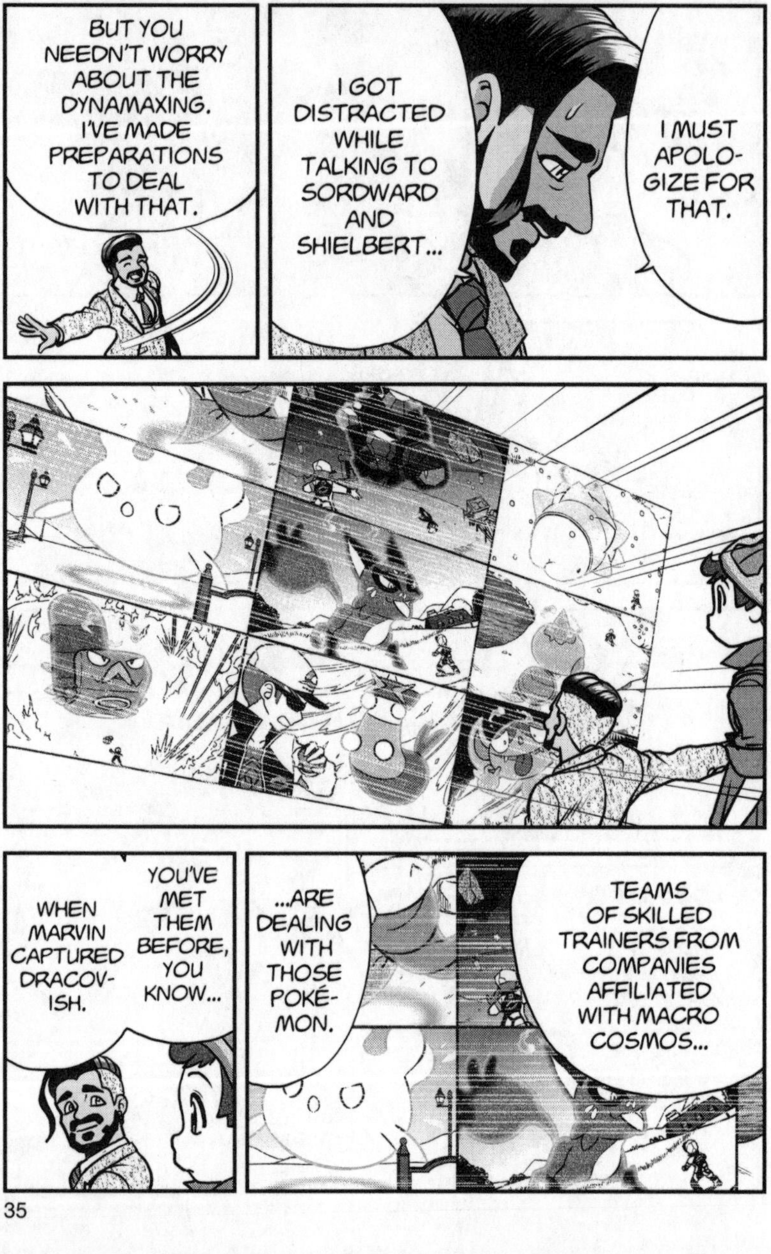
I MUST APOLO-GIZE FOR THAT.
I GOT DISTRACTED WHILE TALKING TO SORDWARD AND SHIELBERT...
BUT YOU NEEDN'T WORRY ABOUT THE DYNAMAXING. I'VE MADE PREPARATIONS TO DEAL WITH THAT.
TEAMS OF SKILLED TRAINERS FROM COMPANIES AFFILIATED WITH MACRO COSMOS...
...ARE DEALING WITH THOSE POKÉ-MON.
YOU'VE MET THEM BEFORE, YOU KNOW...
WHEN MARVIN CAPTURED DRACOV-ISH.

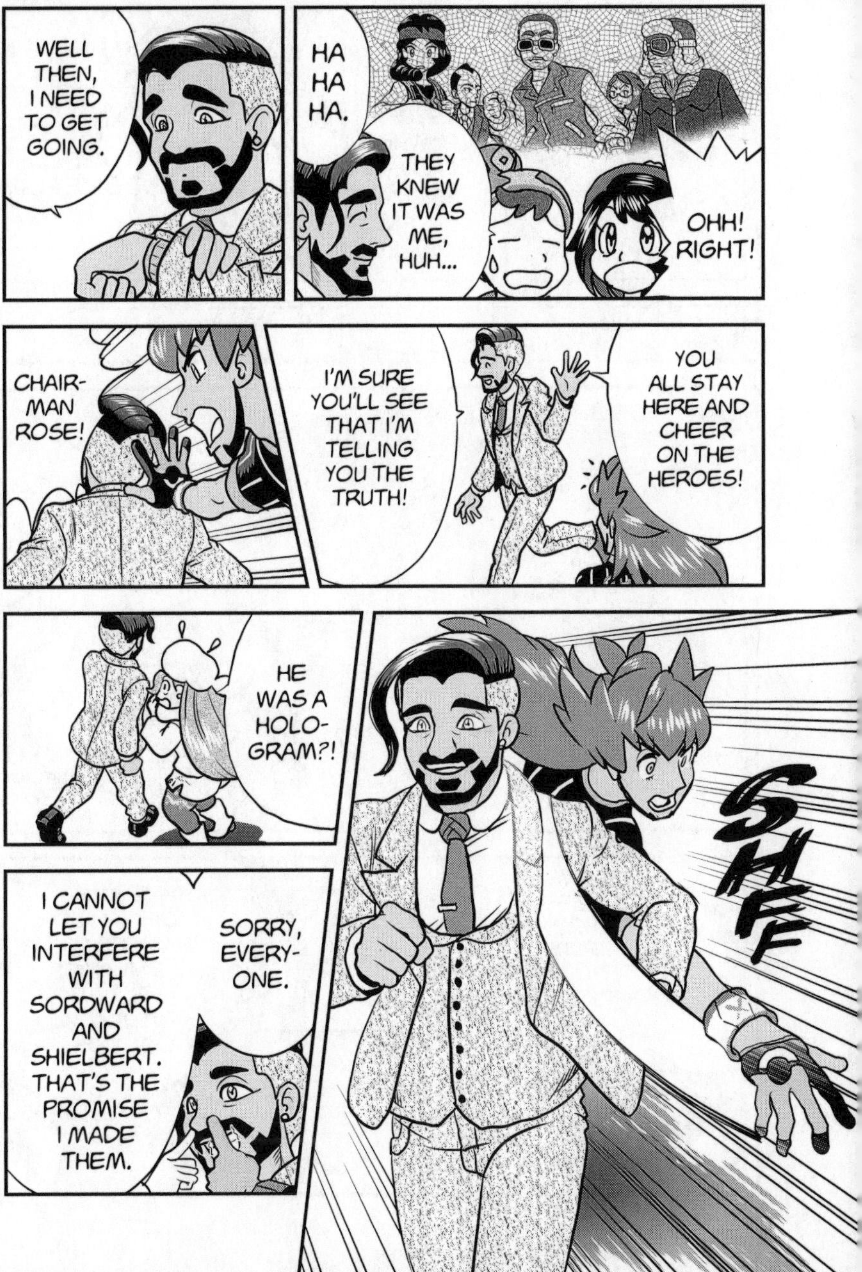
HA HA HA.
THEY KNEW IT WAS ME, HUH...
OHH! RIGHT!
WELL THEN, I NEED TO GET GOING.
YOU ALL STAY HERE AND CHEER ON THE HEROES!
I'M SURE YOU'LL SEE THAT I'M TELLING YOU THE TRUTH!
CHAIR-MAN ROSE!
SHFF
HE WAS A HOLO-GRAM?!
SORRY, EVERY-ONE.
I CANNOT LET YOU INTERFERE WITH SORDWARD AND SHIELBERT. THAT'S THE PROMISE I MADE THEM.

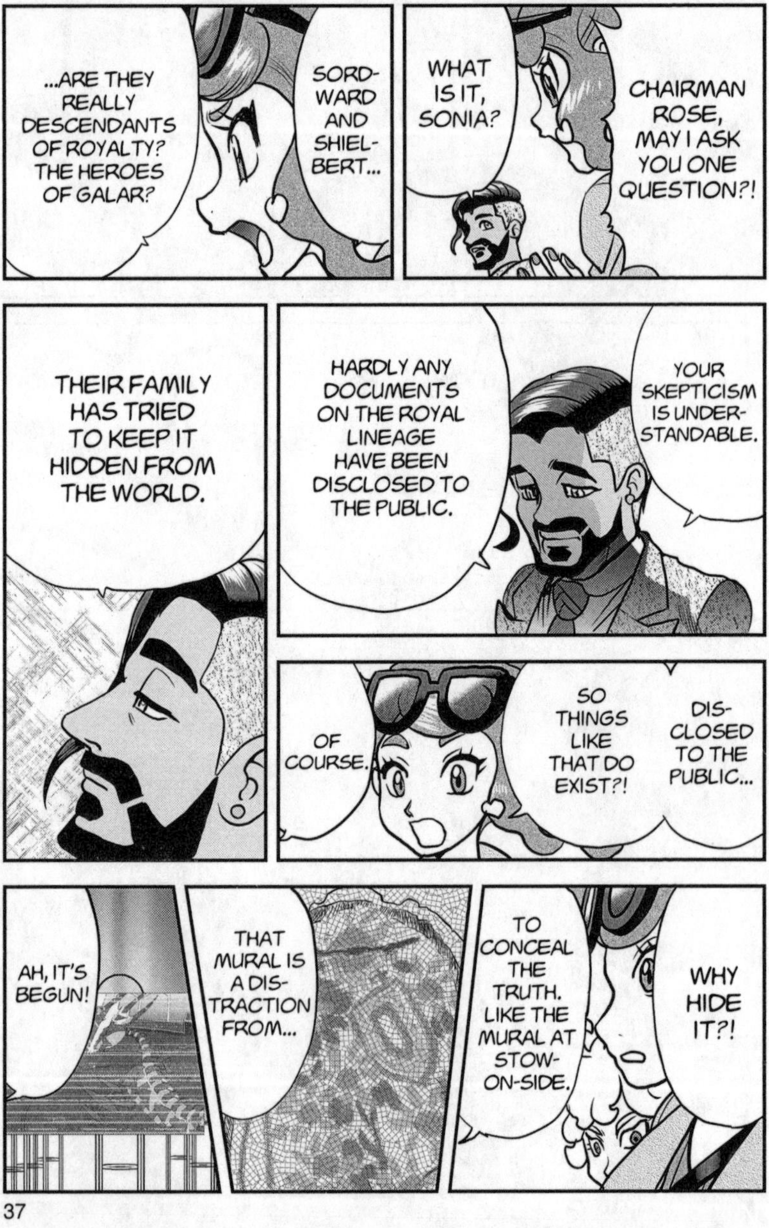
CHAIRMAN ROSE, MAY I ASK YOU ONE QUESTION?!
WHAT IS IT, SONIA?
SORDWARD AND SHIELBERT...
...ARE THEY REALLY DESCENDANTS OF ROYALTY? THE HEROES OF GALAR?
YOUR SKEPTICISM IS UNDERSTANDABLE.
HARDLY ANY DOCUMENTS ON THE ROYAL LINEAGE HAVE BEEN DISCLOSED TO THE PUBLIC.
DISCLOSED TO THE PUBLIC...
SO THINGS LIKE THAT DO EXIST?!
OF COURSE.
THEIR FAMILY HAS TRIED TO KEEP IT HIDDEN FROM THE WORLD.
WHY HIDE IT?!
TO CONCEAL THE TRUTH. LIKE THE MURAL AT STOW-ON-SIDE.
THAT MURAL IS A DISTRACTION FROM...
AH, IT'S BEGUN!

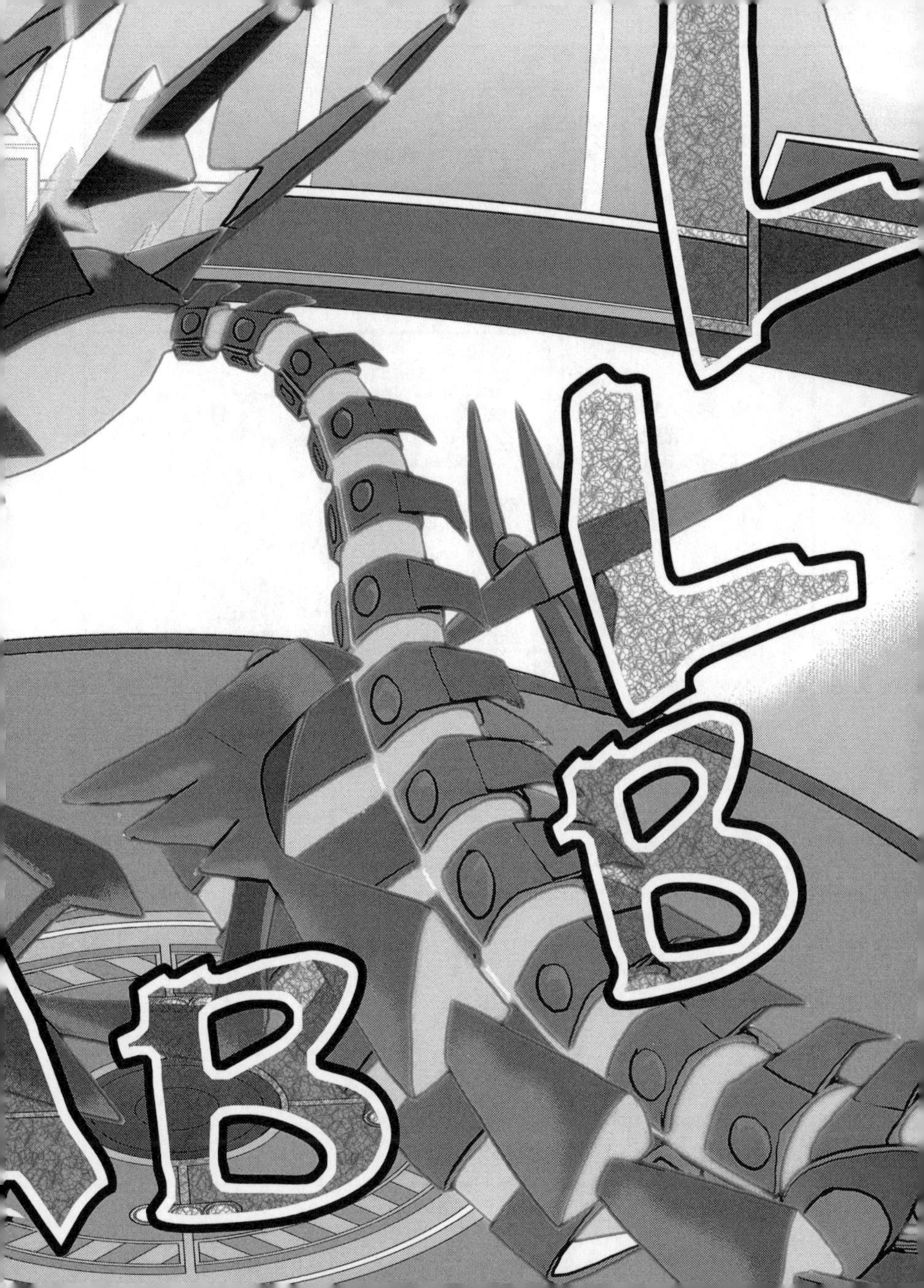
BBLL

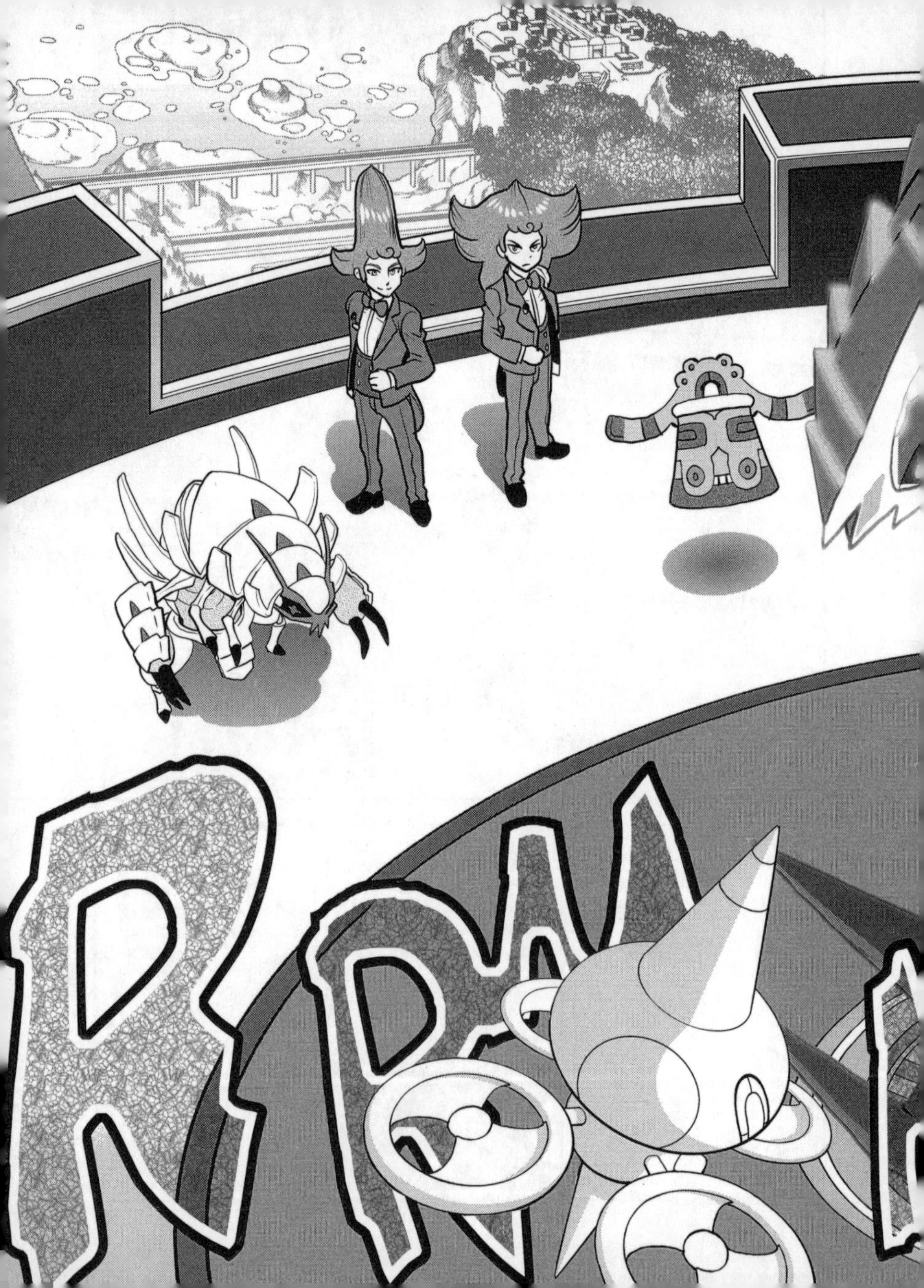

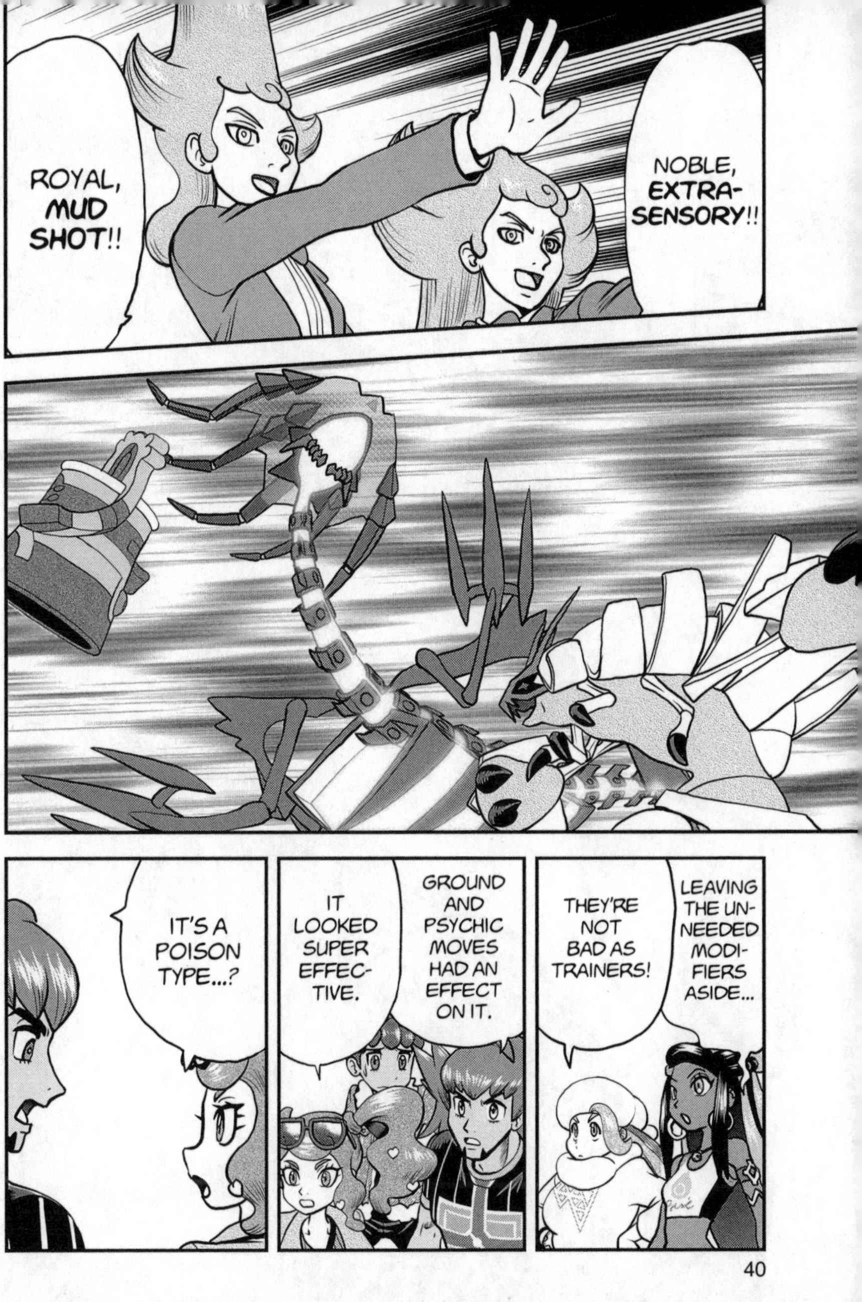
NOBLE, EXTRA-SENSORY!!
ROYAL, MUD SHOT!!
LEAVING THE UN-NEEDED MODI-FIERS ASIDE...
THEY'RE NOT BAD AS TRAINERS!
GROUND AND PSYCHIC MOVES HAD AN EFFECT ON IT.
IT LOOKED SUPER EFFEC-TIVE.
IT'S A POISON TYPE...?

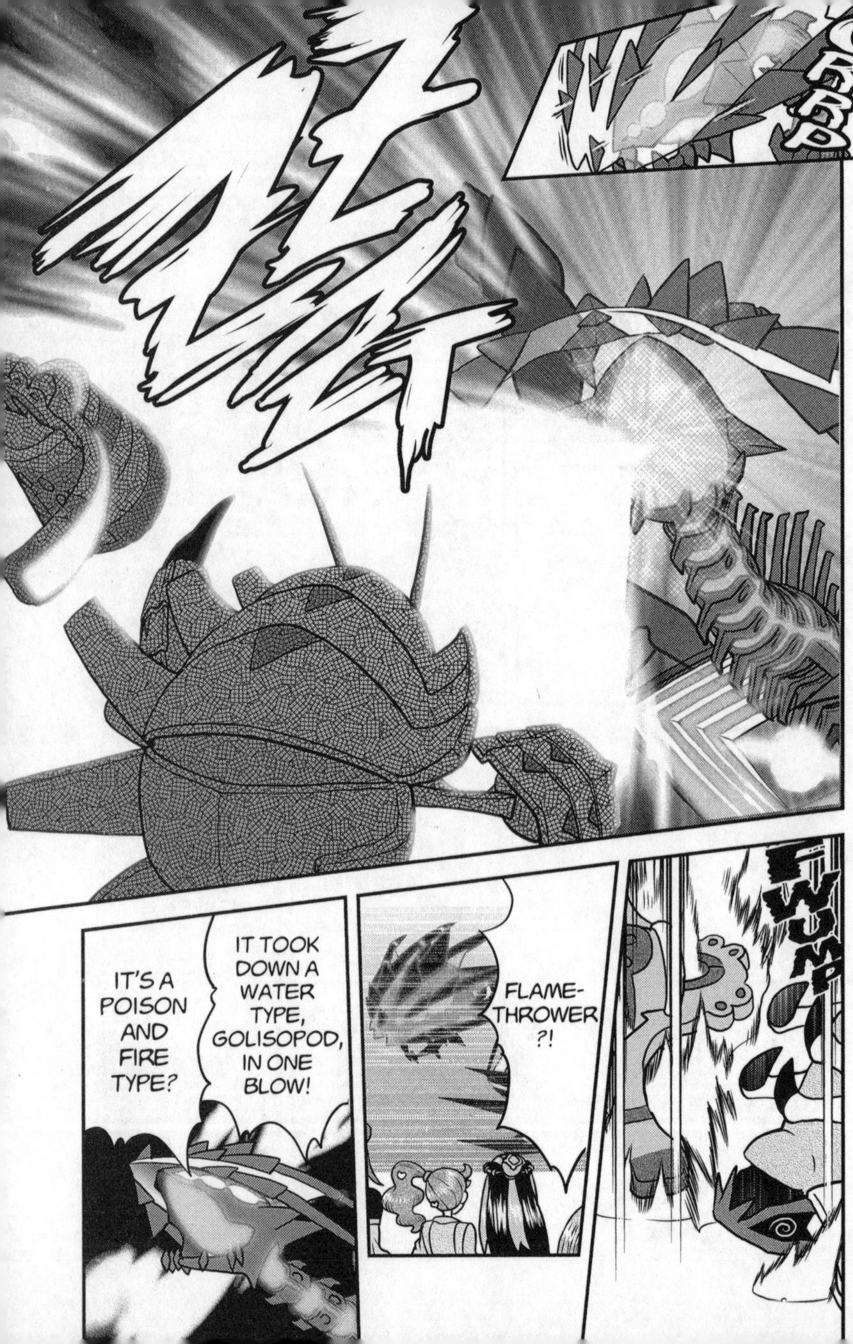
GRRD
WUMP
FLAME-THROWER?!
IT TOOK DOWN A WATER TYPE, GOLISOPOD, IN ONE BLOW!
IT'S A POISON AND FIRE TYPE?

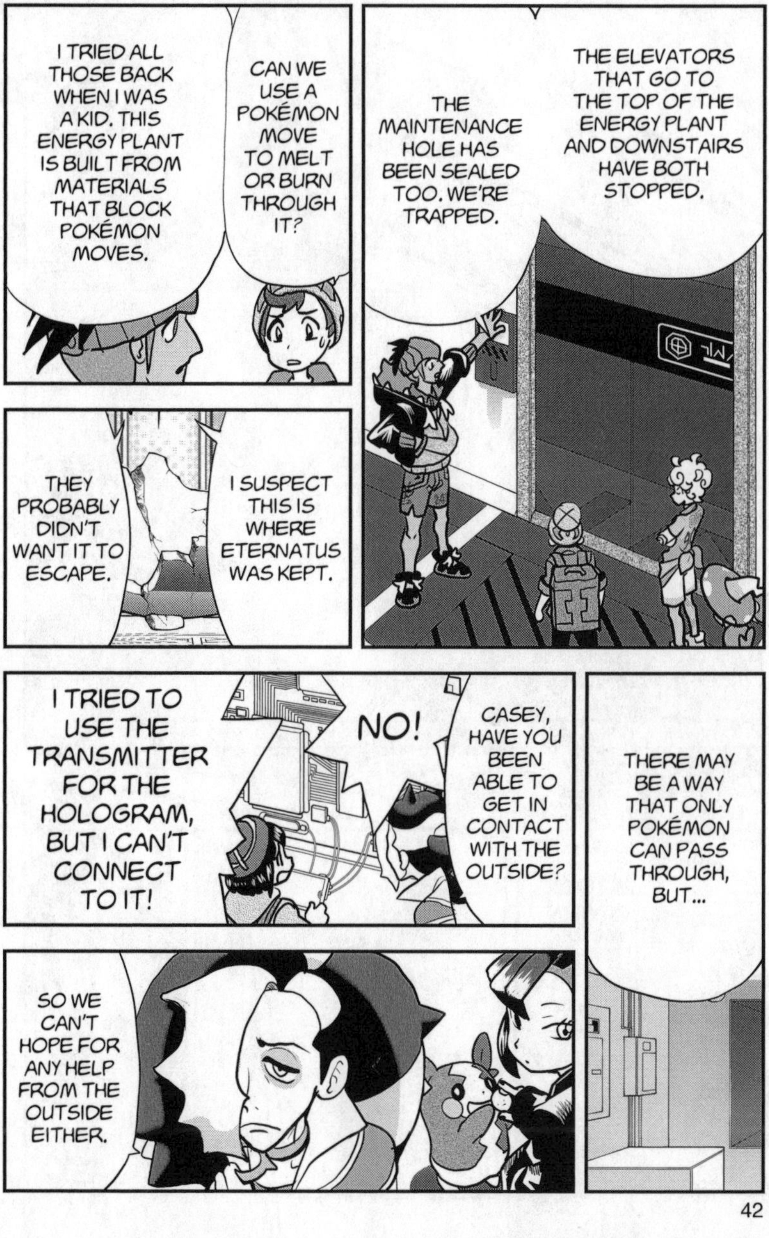
THE ELEVATORS THAT GO TO THE TOP OF THE ENERGY PLANT AND DOWNSTAIRS HAVE BOTH STOPPED.
THE MAINTENANCE HOLE HAS BEEN SEALED TOO. WE'RE TRAPPED.
CAN WE USE A POKÉMON MOVE TO MELT OR BURN THROUGH IT?
I TRIED ALL THOSE BACK WHEN I WAS A KID. THIS ENERGY PLANT IS BUILT FROM MATERIALS THAT BLOCK POKÉMON MOVES.
I SUSPECT THIS IS WHERE ETERNATUS WAS KEPT.
THEY PROBABLY DIDN'T WANT IT TO ESCAPE.
THERE MAY BE A WAY THAT ONLY POKÉMON CAN PASS THROUGH, BUT...
CASEY, HAVE YOU BEEN ABLE TO GET IN CONTACT WITH THE OUTSIDE?
NO!
I TRIED TO USE THE TRANSMITTER FOR THE HOLOGRAM, BUT I CAN'T CONNECT TO IT!
SO WE CAN'T HOPE FOR ANY HELP FROM THE OUTSIDE EITHER.

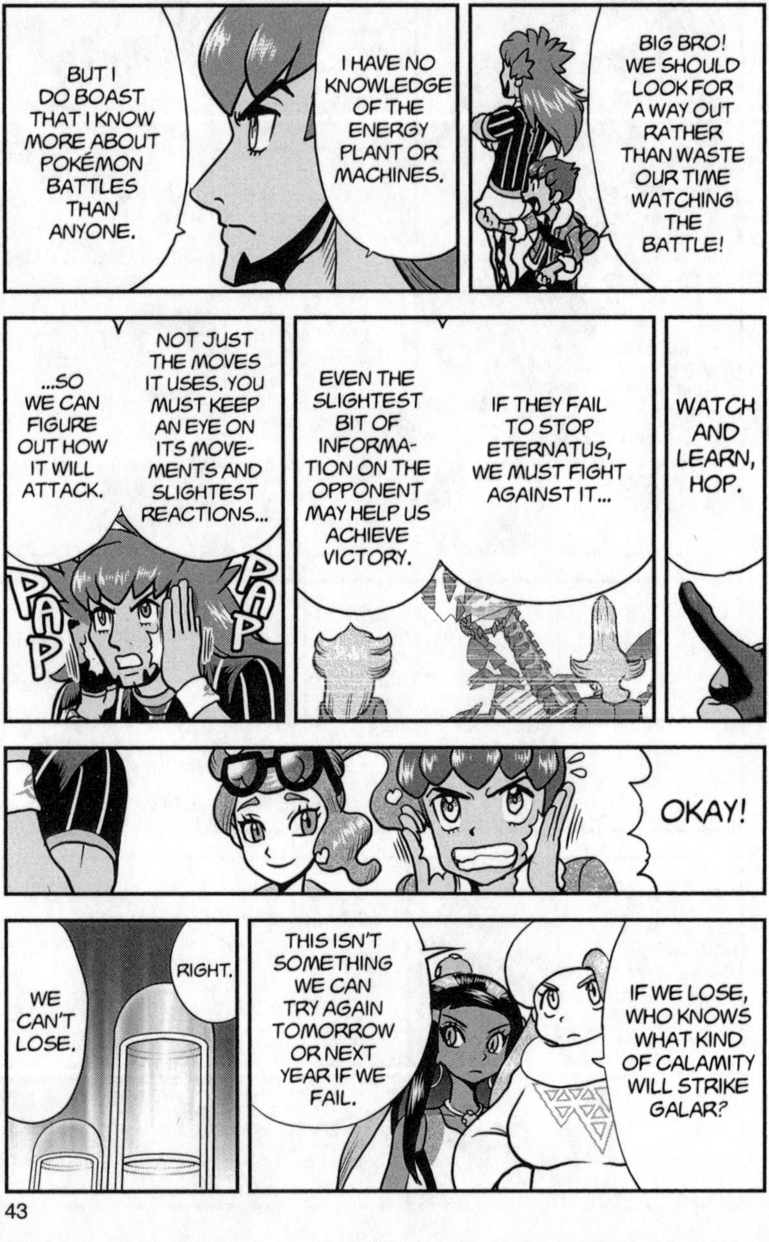
BIG BRO! WE SHOULD LOOK FOR A WAY OUT RATHER THAN WASTE OUR TIME WATCHING THE BATTLE!
I HAVE NO KNOWLEDGE OF THE ENERGY PLANT OR MACHINES.
BUT I DO BOAST THAT I KNOW MORE ABOUT POKÉMON BATTLES THAN ANYONE.
WATCH AND LEARN, HOP.
IF THEY FAIL TO STOP ETERNATUS, WE MUST FIGHT AGAINST IT...
EVEN THE SLIGHTEST BIT OF INFORMA-TION ON THE OPPONENT MAY HELP US ACHIEVE VICTORY.
NOT JUST THE MOVES IT USES. YOU MUST KEEP AN EYE ON ITS MOVE-MENTS AND SLIGHTEST REACTIONS...
...SO WE CAN FIGURE OUT HOW IT WILL ATTACK.
PAP PAP
PAP PAP
OKAY!
IF WE LOSE, WHO KNOWS WHAT KIND OF CALAMITY WILL STRIKE GALAR?
THIS ISN'T SOMETHING WE CAN TRY AGAIN TOMORROW OR NEXT YEAR IF WE FAIL.
RIGHT.
WE CAN'T LOSE.

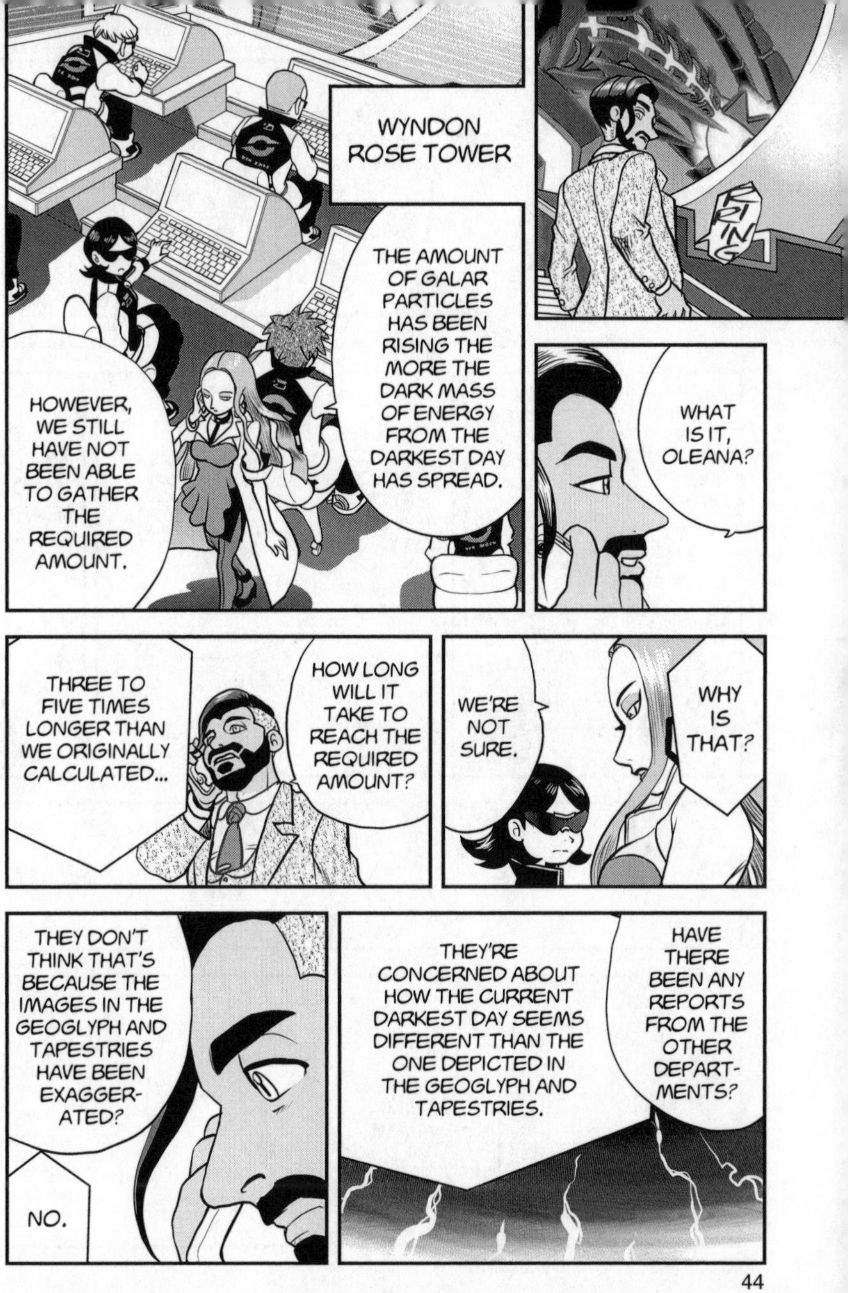
RRING
WHAT IS IT, OLEANA?
WYNDON ROSE TOWER
THE AMOUNT OF GALAR PARTICLES HAS BEEN RISING THE MORE THE DARK MASS OF ENERGY FROM THE DARKEST DAY HAS SPREAD.
HOWEVER, WE STILL HAVE NOT BEEN ABLE TO GATHER THE REQUIRED AMOUNT.
WHY IS THAT?
WE'RE NOT SURE.
HOW LONG WILL IT TAKE TO REACH THE REQUIRED AMOUNT?
THREE TO FIVE TIMES LONGER THAN WE ORIGINALLY CALCULATED...
HAVE THERE BEEN ANY REPORTS FROM THE OTHER DEPART-MENTS?
THEY'RE CONCERNED ABOUT HOW THE CURRENT DARKEST DAY SEEMS DIFFERENT THAN THE ONE DEPICTED IN THE GEOGLYPH AND TAPESTRIES.
THEY DON'T THINK THAT'S BECAUSE THE IMAGES IN THE GEOGLYPH AND TAPESTRIES HAVE BEEN EXAGGER-ATED?
NO.

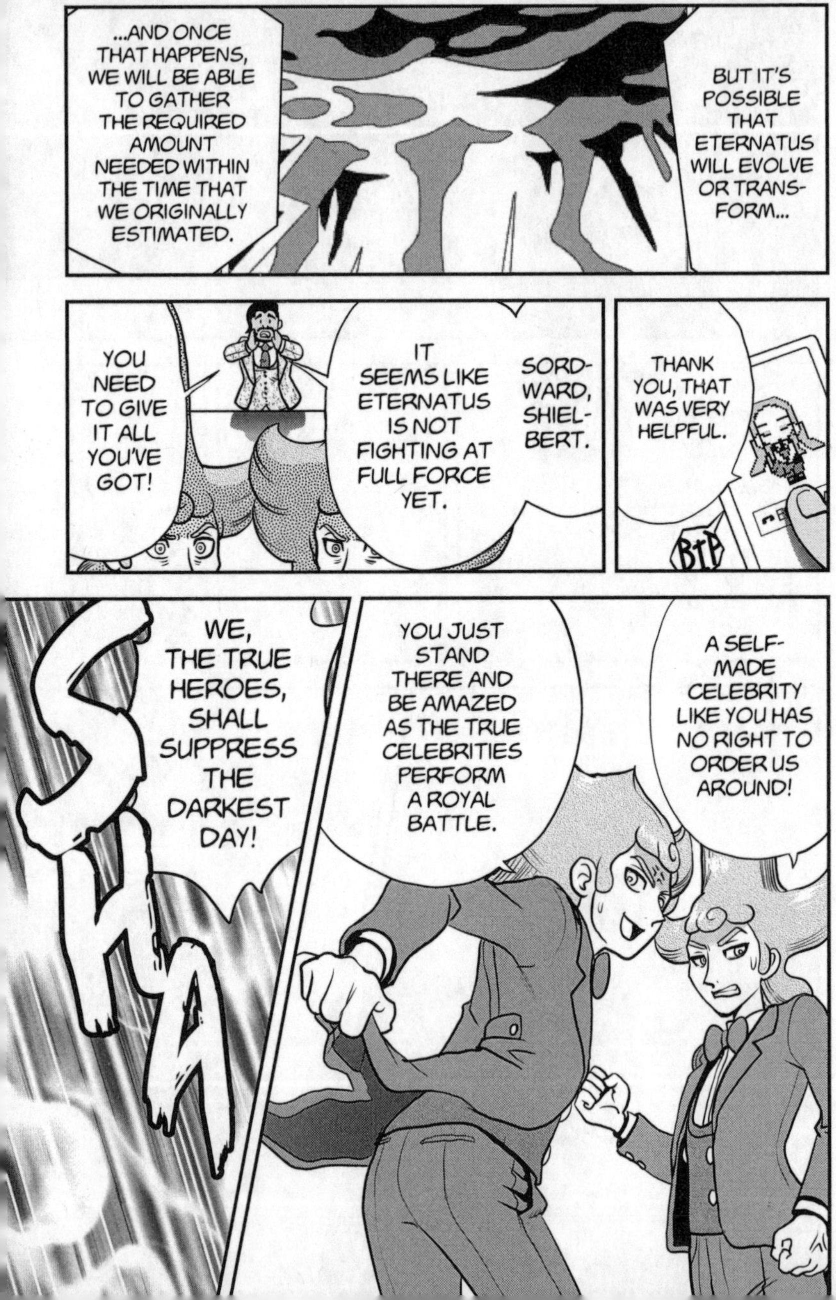
BUT IT'S POSSIBLE THAT ETERNATUS WILL EVOLVE OR TRANS-FORM...
...AND ONCE THAT HAPPENS, WE WILL BE ABLE TO GATHER THE REQUIRED AMOUNT NEEDED WITHIN THE TIME THAT WE ORIGINALLY ESTIMATED.
THANK YOU, THAT WAS VERY HELPFUL.
SORD-WARD, SHIEL-BERT.
IT SEEMS LIKE ETERNATUS IS NOT FIGHTING AT FULL FORCE YET.
YOU NEED TO GIVE IT ALL YOU'VE GOT!
A SELF-MADE CELEBRITY LIKE YOU HAS NO RIGHT TO ORDER US AROUND!
YOU JUST STAND THERE AND BE AMAZED AS THE TRUE CELEBRITIES PERFORM A ROYAL BATTLE.
WE, THE TRUE HEROES, SHALL SUPPRESS THE DARKEST DAY!
SHA

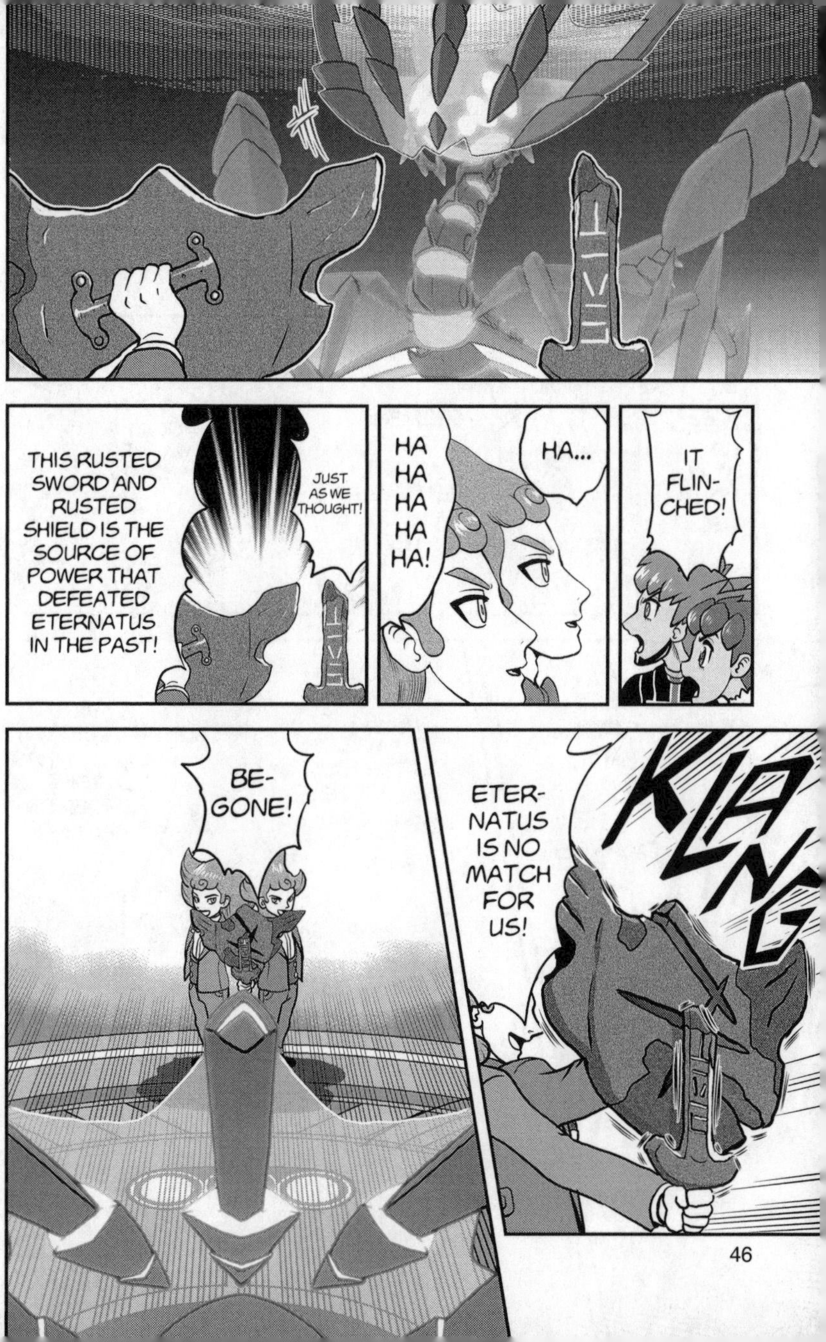
IT FLIN-CHED!
HA...
HA HA HA HA HA!
JUST AS WE THOUGHT!
THIS RUSTED SWORD AND RUSTED SHIELD IS THE SOURCE OF POWER THAT DEFEATED ETERNATUS IN THE PAST!
KLANG
ETER-NATUS IS NO MATCH FOR US!
BE-GONE!

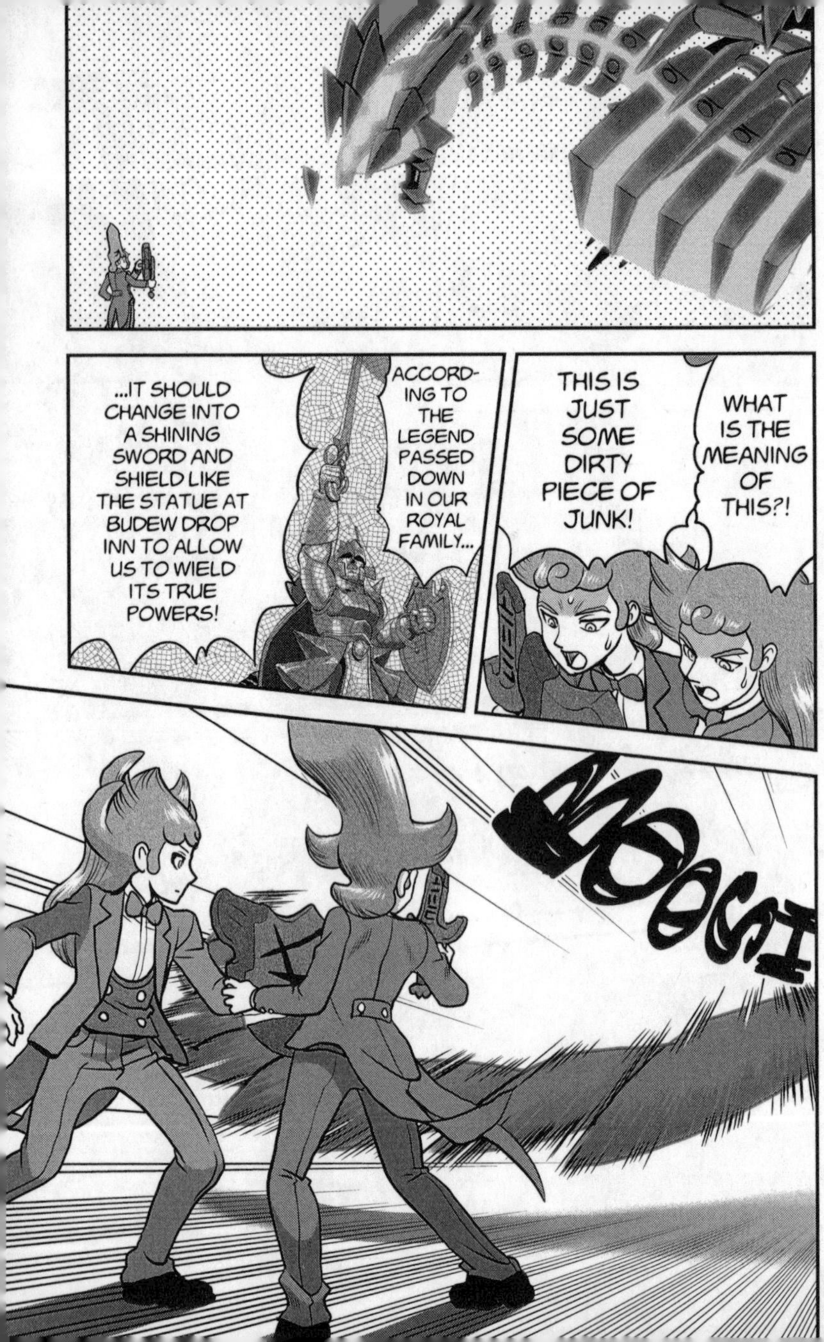
WHAT IS THE MEANING OF THIS?!
THIS IS JUST SOME DIRTY PIECE OF JUNK!
ACCORDING TO THE LEGEND PASSED DOWN IN OUR ROYAL FAMILY...
...IT SHOULD CHANGE INTO A SHINING SWORD AND SHIELD LIKE THE STATUE AT BUDEW DROP INN TO ALLOW US TO WIELD ITS TRUE POWERS!

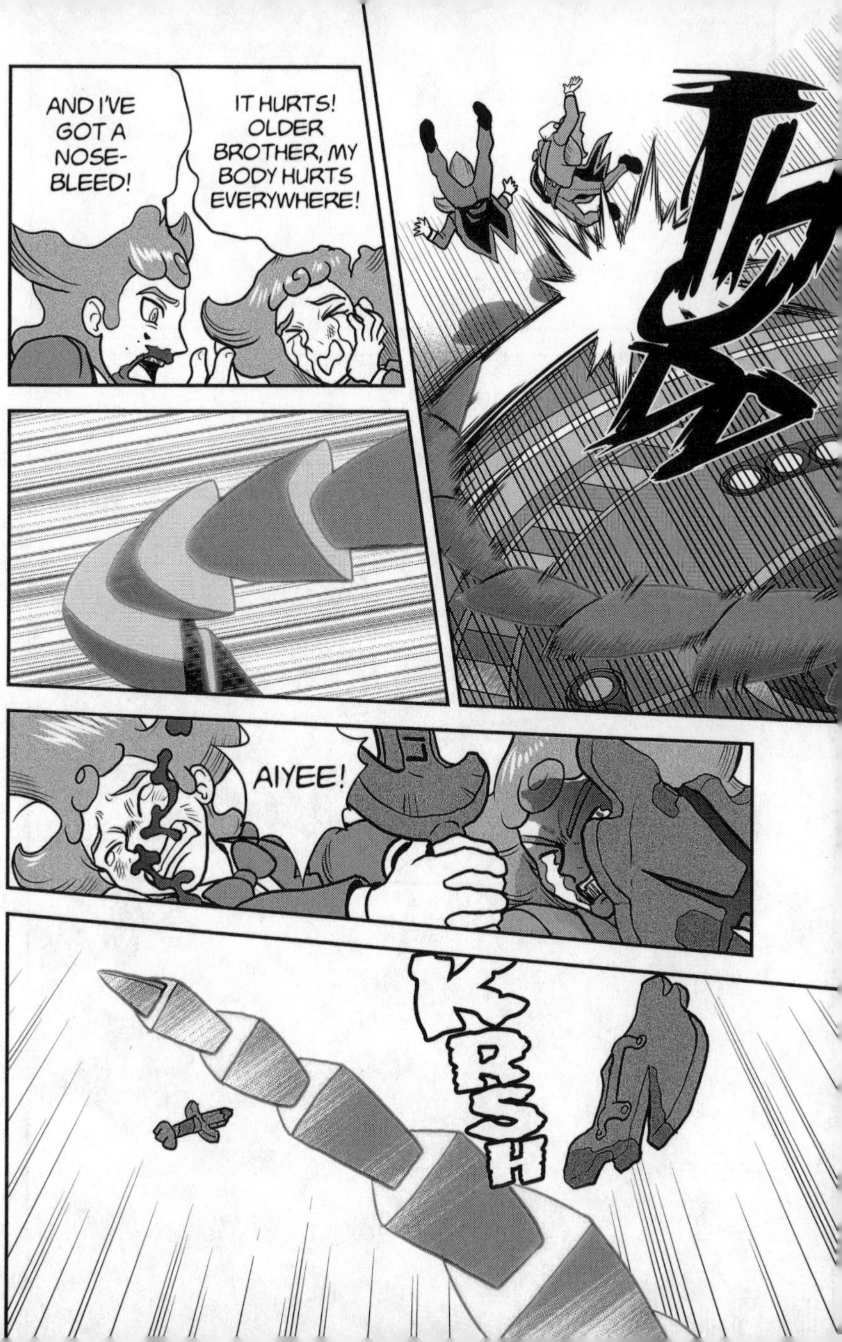
IT HURTS! OLDER BROTHER, MY BODY HURTS EVERYWHERE!
AND I'VE GOT A NOSE-BLEED!
AIYEE!
KRSH

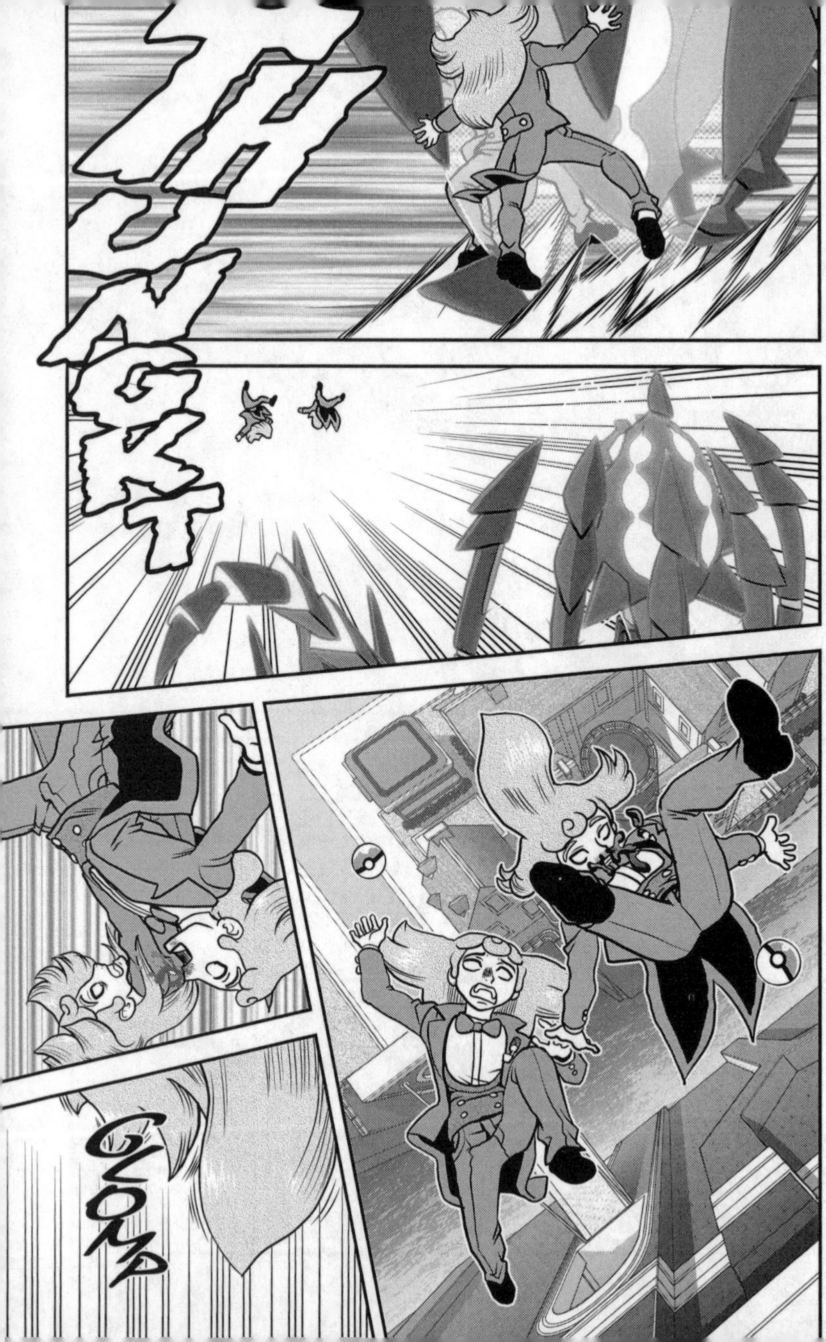
GLOMP

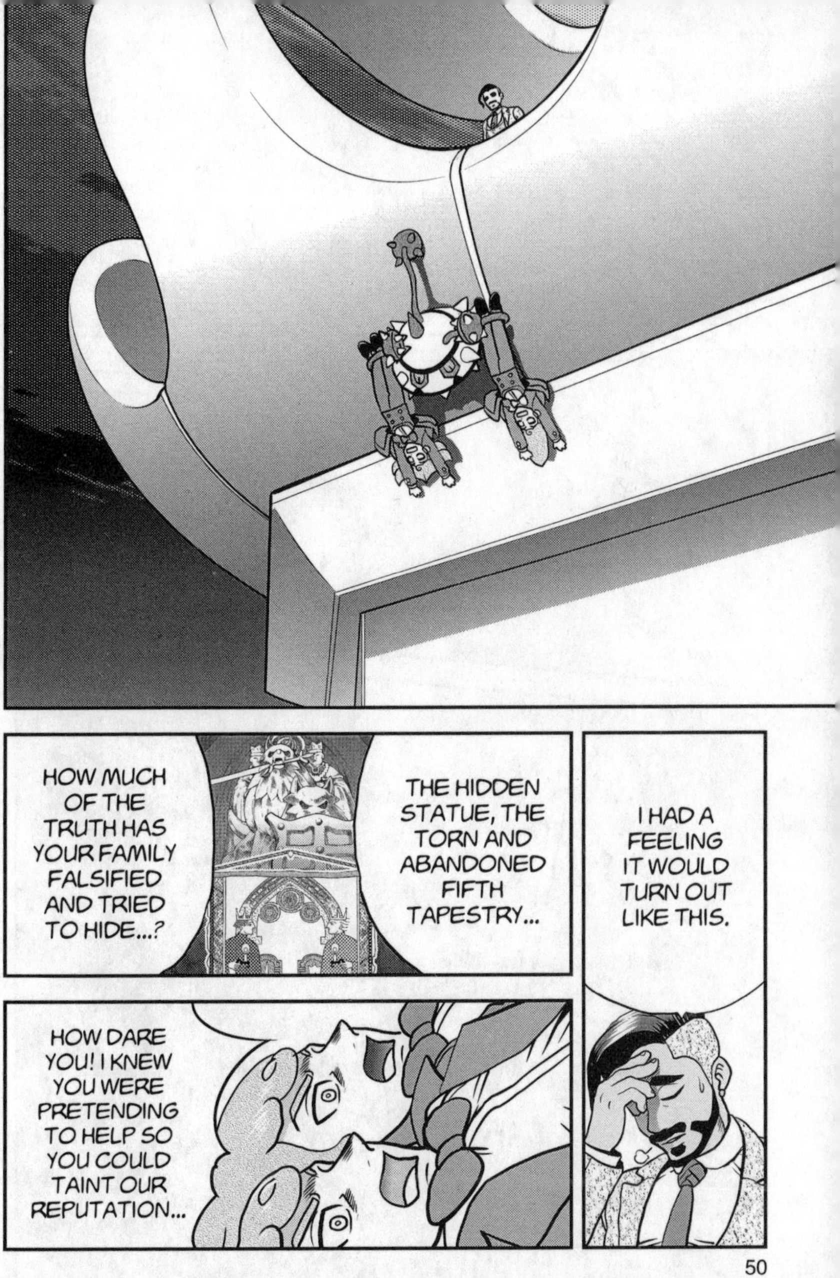
I HAD A FEELING IT WOULD TURN OUT LIKE THIS.
THE HIDDEN STATUE, THE TORN AND ABANDONED FIFTH TAPESTRY...
HOW MUCH OF THE TRUTH HAS YOUR FAMILY FALSIFIED AND TRIED TO HIDE...?
HOW DARE YOU! I KNEW YOU WERE PRETENDING TO HELP SO YOU COULD TAINT OUR REPUTATION...

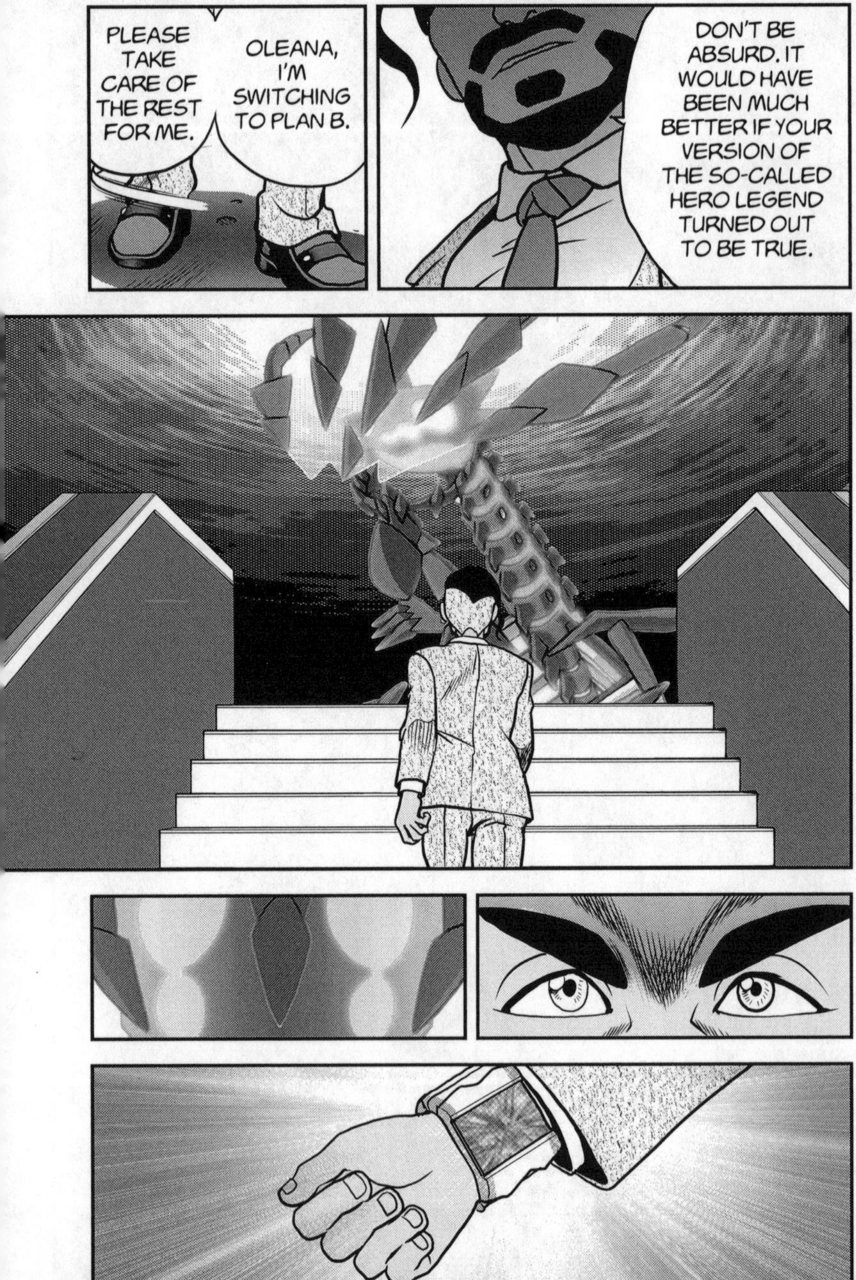
DON'T BE ABSURD. IT WOULD HAVE BEEN MUCH BETTER IF YOUR VERSION OF THE SO-CALLED HERO LEGEND TURNED OUT TO BE TRUE.
OLEANA, I'M SWITCHING TO PLAN B.
PLEASE TAKE CARE OF THE REST FOR ME.

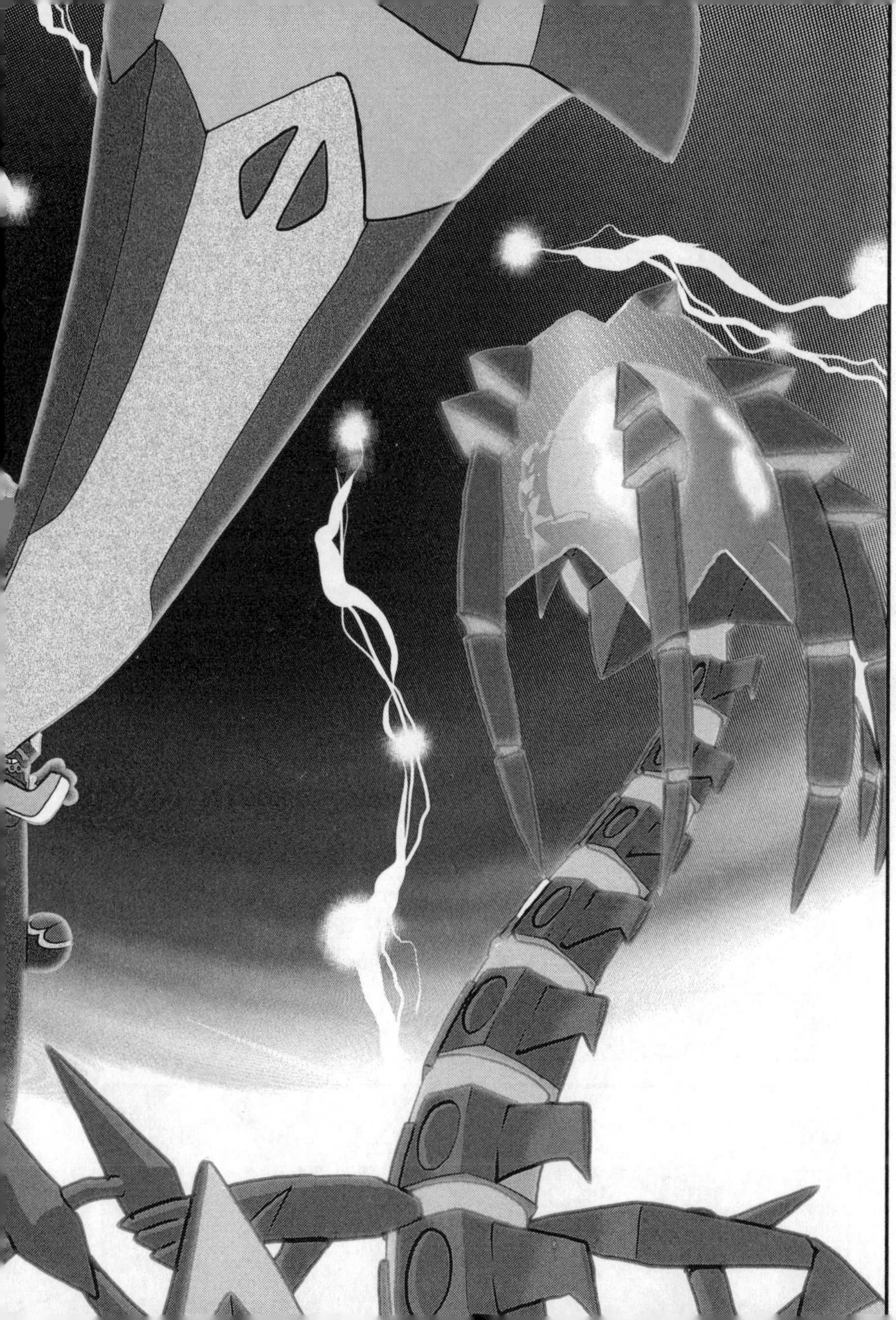

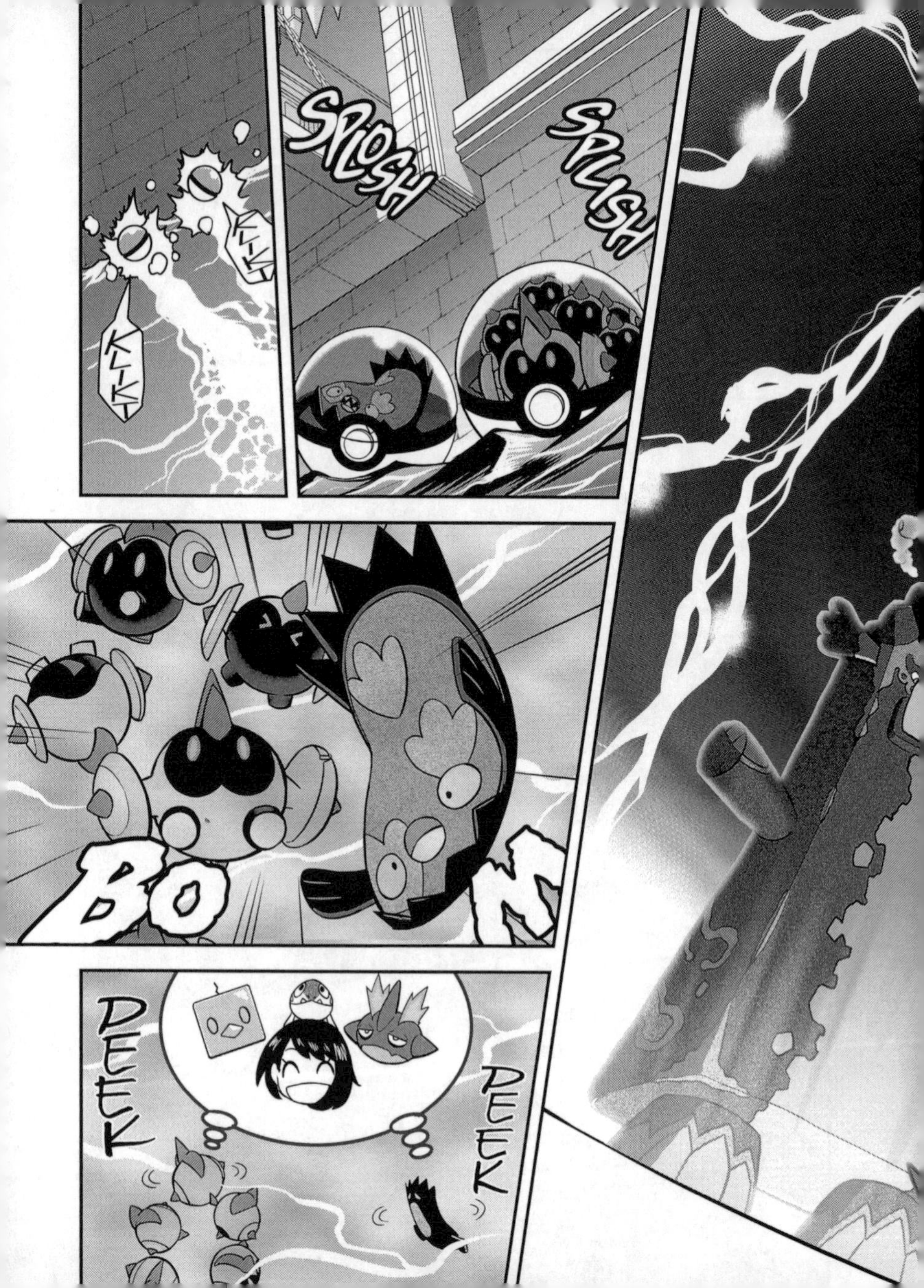
SPLOSH
SPLISH
KLIKT
KLIKT
BO M
DEEEK
DEEEK

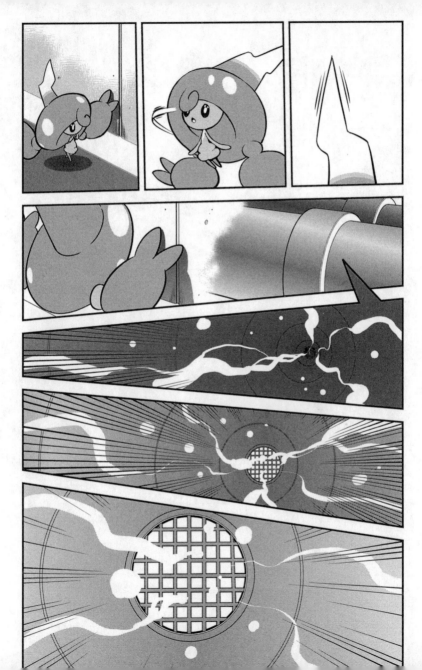

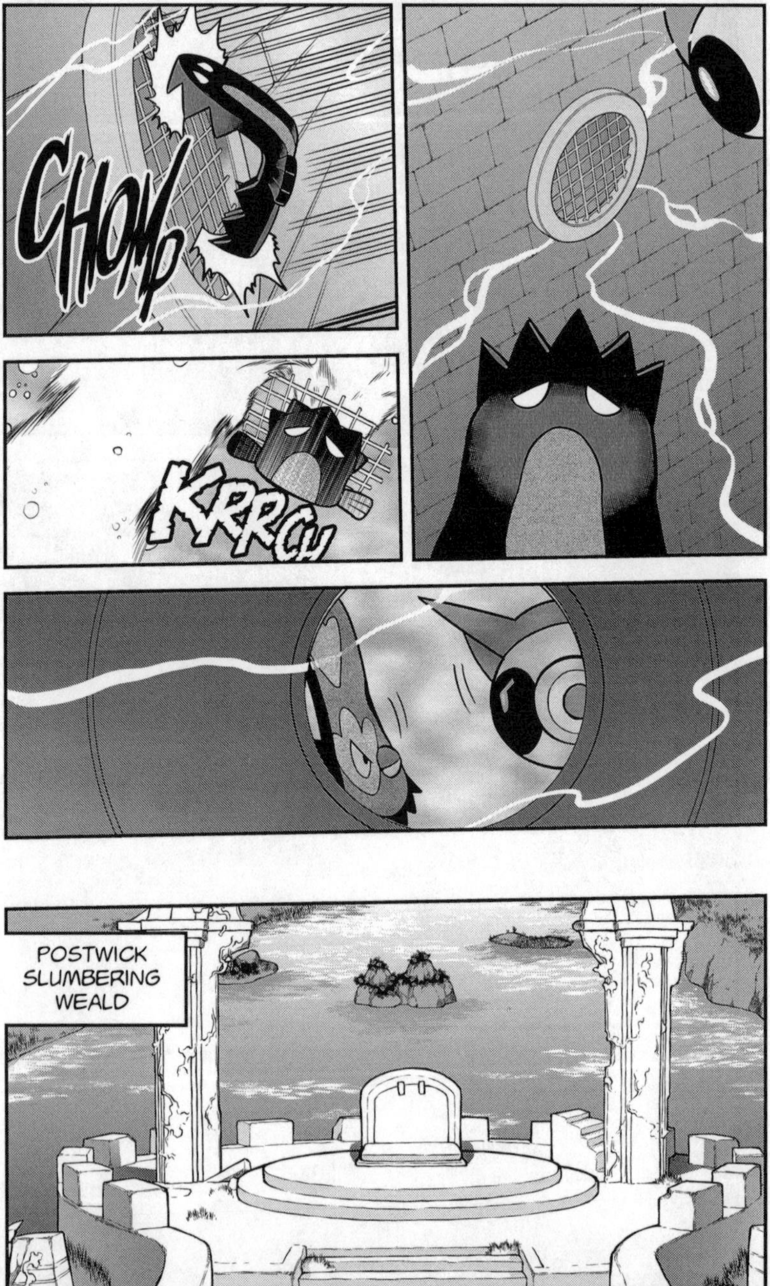
CHOMP
KRRCH
POSTWICK
SLUMBERING
WEALD

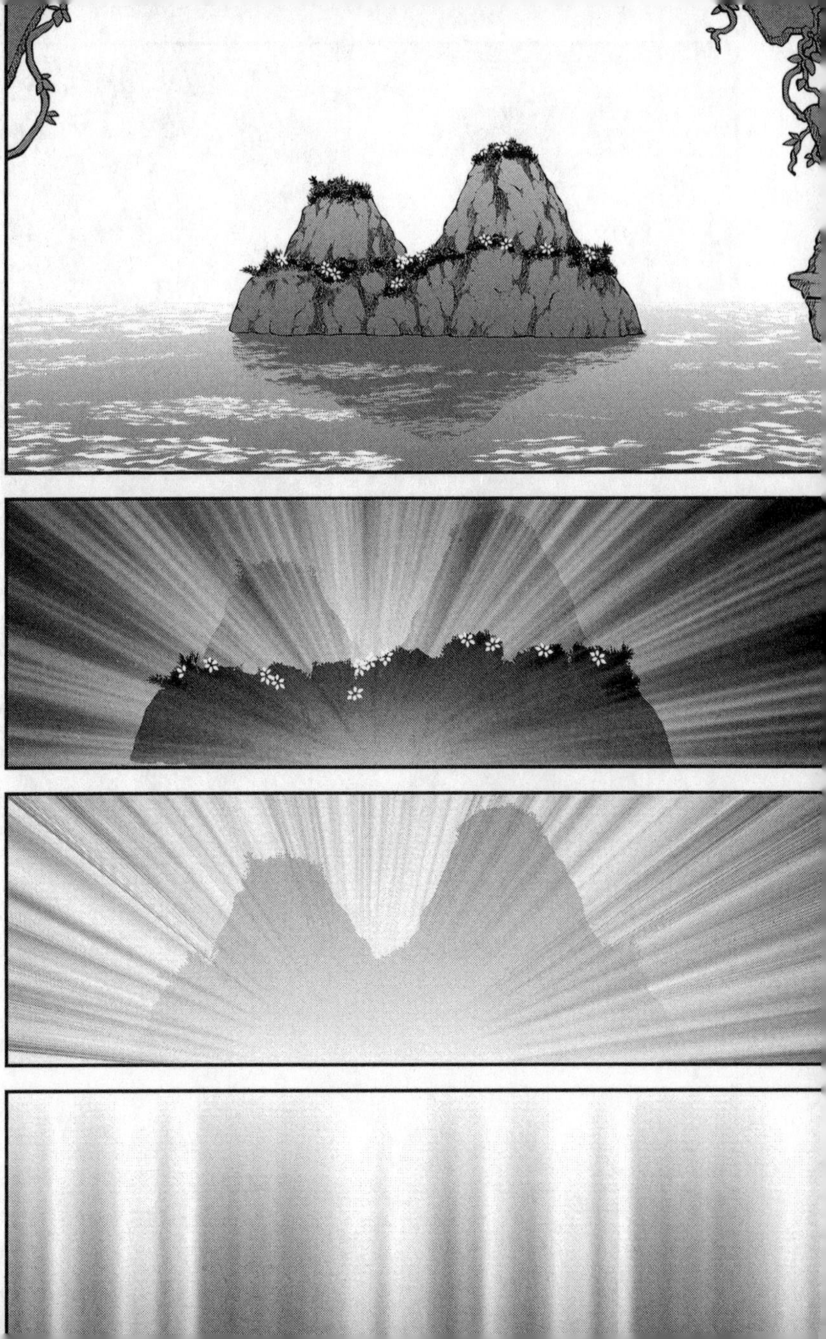

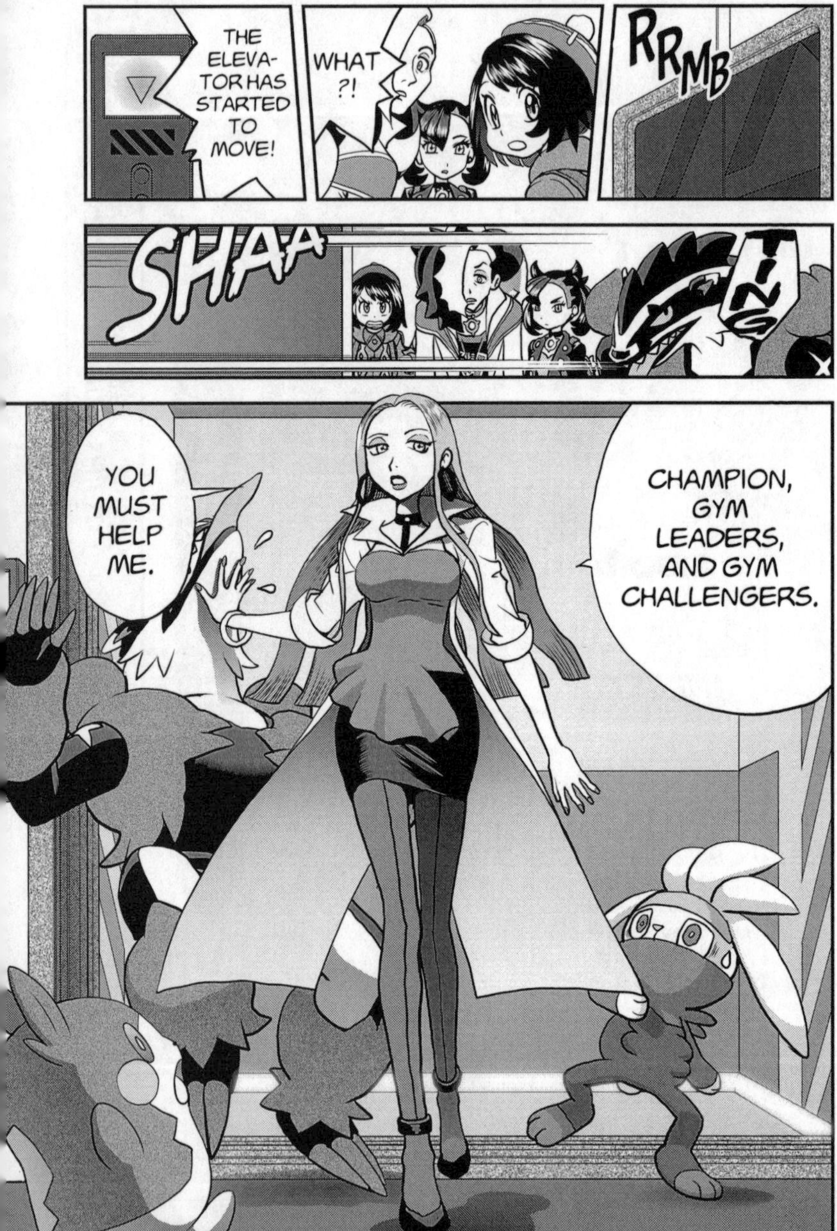
RRMB
WHAT?!
THE ELEVA-TOR HAS STARTED TO MOVE!
TING
SHAA
CHAMPION, GYM LEADERS, AND GYM CHALLENGERS.
YOU MUST HELP ME.

GIGANTAMAX ALCREMIE

TYPE	Fairy
ABILITY	Sweet Veil
G-MAX MOVE	G-Max Finale

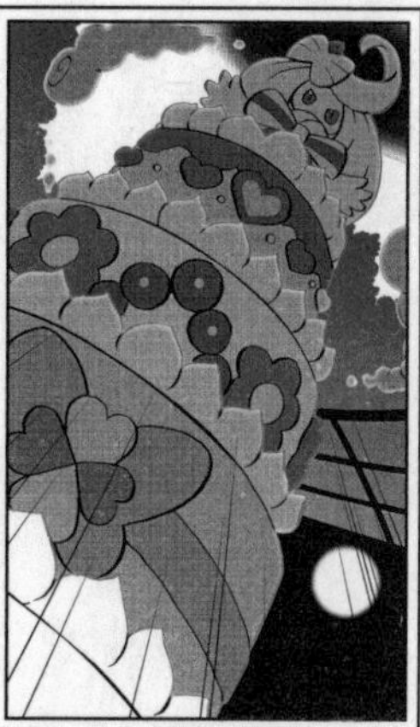

HEIGHT	98'05"+
WEIGHT	??? lbs

ORDINARY

ALCREMIE

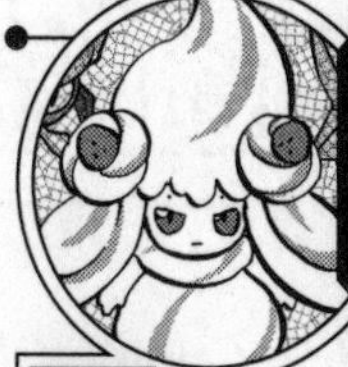

HEIGHT	1'00"
WEIGHT	1.1 lbs

Alcremie have various sweet forms and flavors, but they will all change into the same Gigantamax form. It looks like a giant cake and can be very imposing. Its missile-like cream attack is powerful too!!

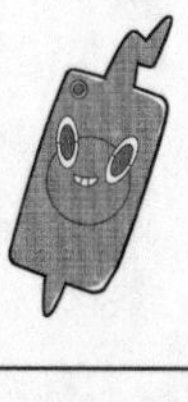

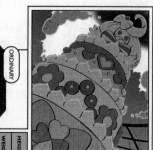

STRATEGY NOTES

The Fairy-type move used by a Gigantamax Alcremie is G-Max Finale. It's a tricky move that will attack its opponent while healing its allies. Also, the cream that pours out of its body endlessly stiffens upon impact. Is there a way to defeat it?!

Adventure 28 Splash!! The Return of the Two Pokémon

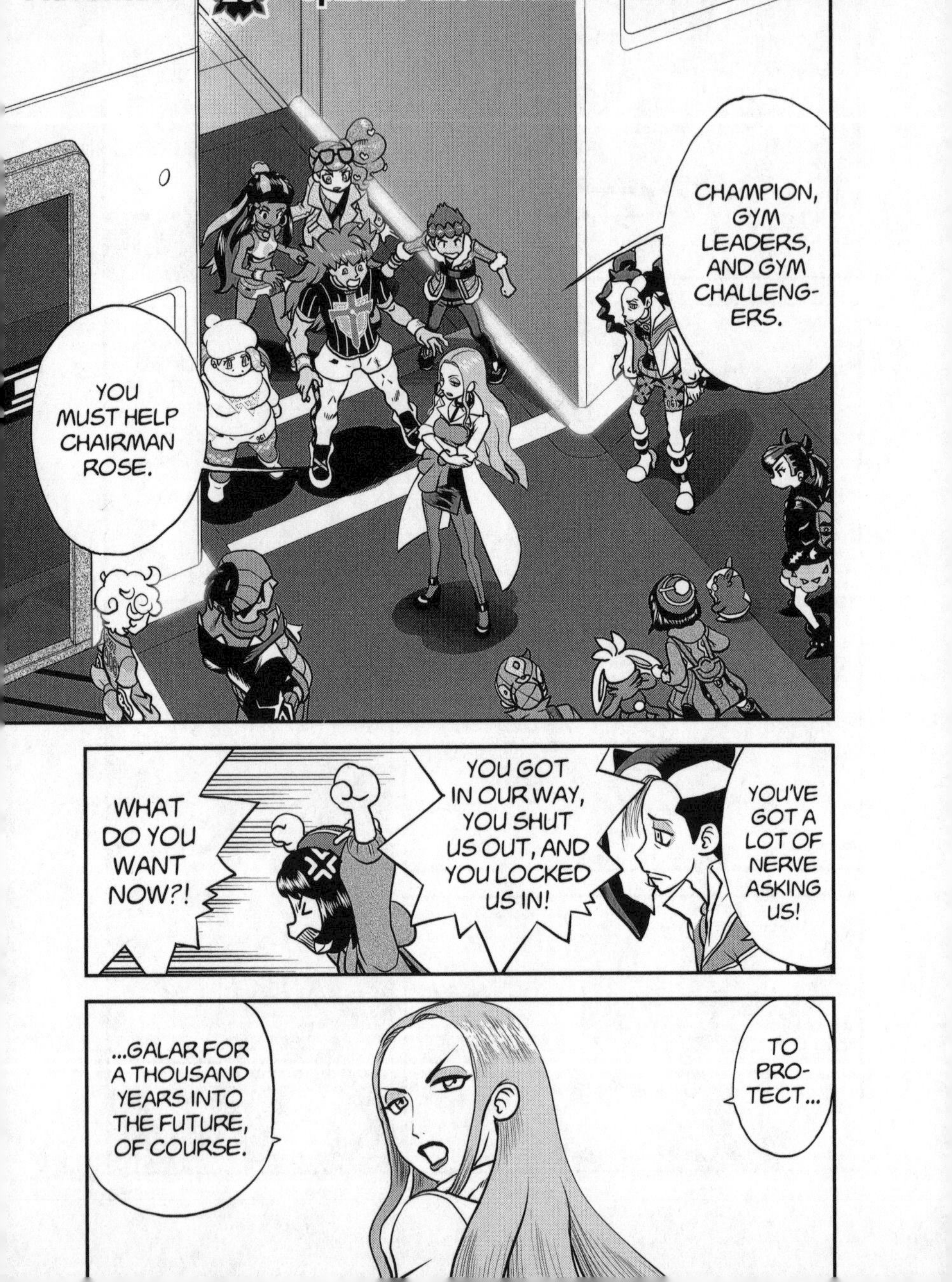
CHAMPION, GYM LEADERS, AND GYM CHALLENG-ERS.
YOU MUST HELP CHAIRMAN ROSE.
YOU'VE GOT A LOT OF NERVE ASKING US!
YOU GOT IN OUR WAY, YOU SHUT US OUT, AND YOU LOCKED US IN!
WHAT DO YOU WANT NOW?!
TO PRO-TECT...
...GALAR FOR A THOUSAND YEARS INTO THE FUTURE, OF COURSE.

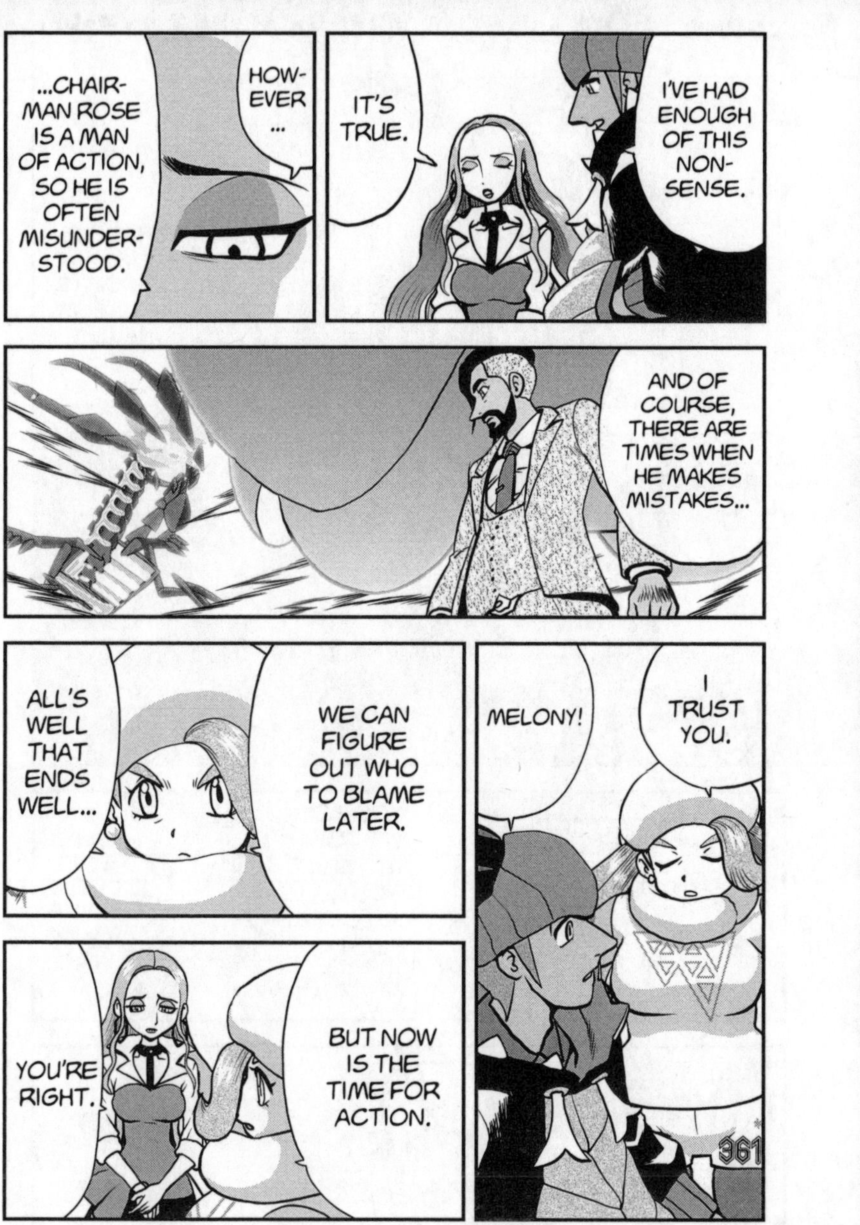
I'VE HAD ENOUGH OF THIS NON-SENSE.
IT'S TRUE.
HOW-EVER ...
...CHAIR-MAN ROSE IS A MAN OF ACTION, SO HE IS OFTEN MISUNDER-STOOD.
AND OF COURSE, THERE ARE TIMES WHEN HE MAKES MISTAKES...
I TRUST YOU.
MELONY!
361
WE CAN FIGURE OUT WHO TO BLAME LATER.
ALL'S WELL THAT ENDS WELL...
BUT NOW IS THE TIME FOR ACTION.
YOU'RE RIGHT.

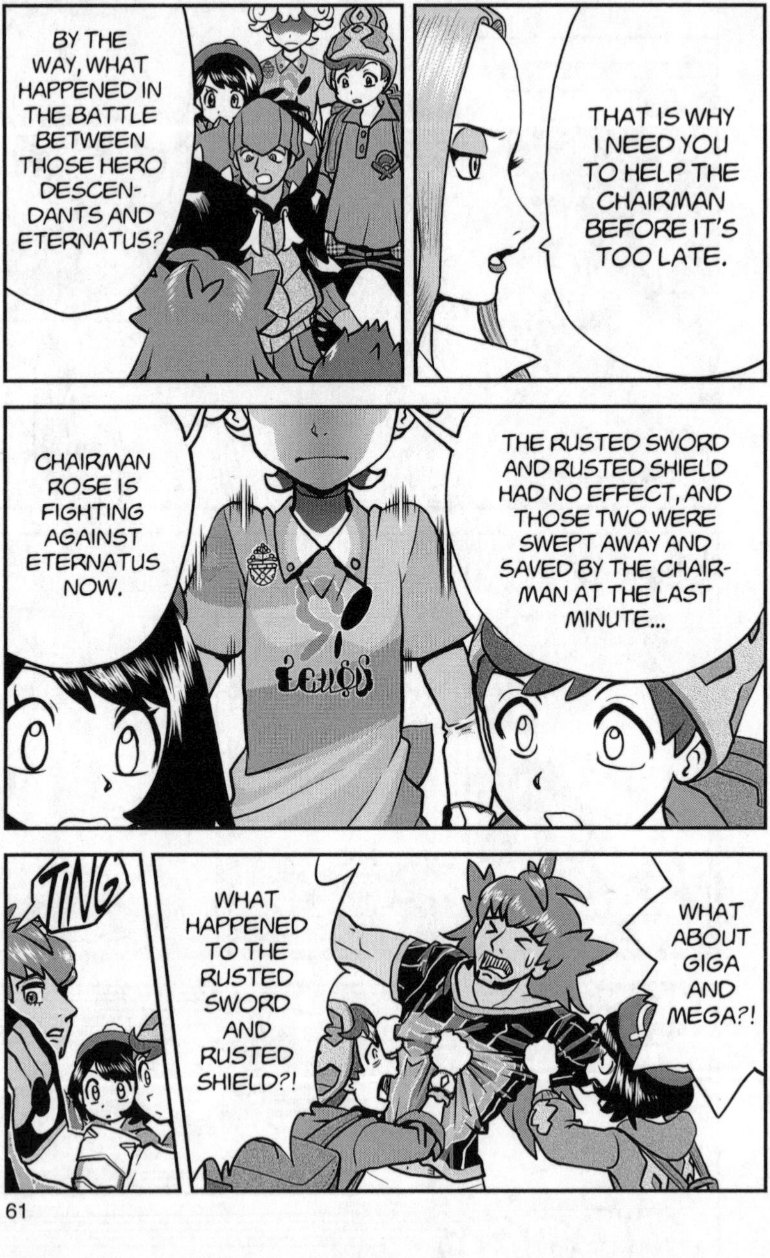
THAT IS WHY I NEED YOU TO HELP THE CHAIRMAN BEFORE IT'S TOO LATE.
BY THE WAY, WHAT HAPPENED IN THE BATTLE BETWEEN THOSE HERO DESCEN-DANTS AND ETERNATUS?
THE RUSTED SWORD AND RUSTED SHIELD HAD NO EFFECT, AND THOSE TWO WERE SWEPT AWAY AND SAVED BY THE CHAIR-MAN AT THE LAST MINUTE...
CHAIRMAN ROSE IS FIGHTING AGAINST ETERNATUS NOW.
WHAT ABOUT GIGA AND MEGA?!
WHAT HAPPENED TO THE RUSTED SWORD AND RUSTED SHIELD?!
TING

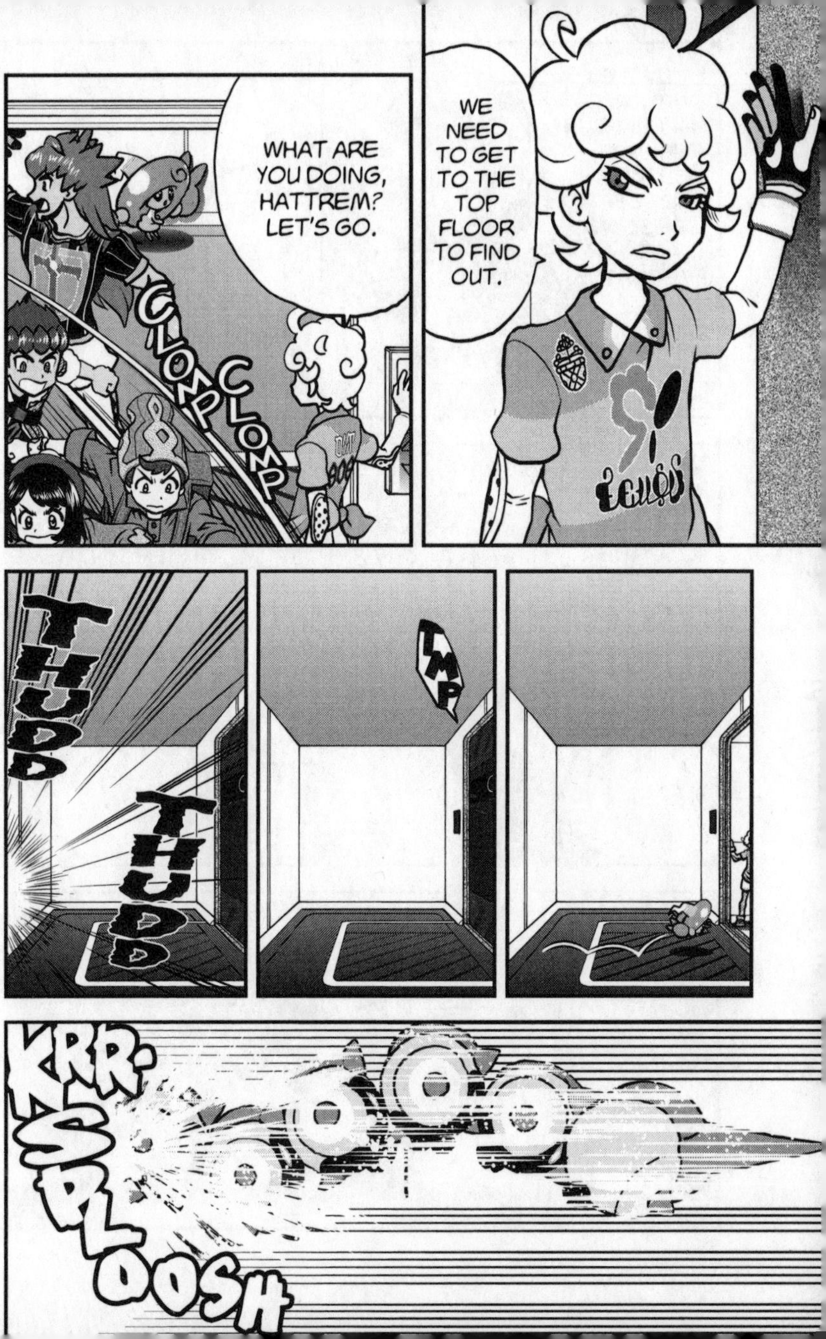
WE NEED TO GET TO THE TOP FLOOR TO FIND OUT.
WHAT ARE YOU DOING, HATTREM? LET'S GO.
CLOMP CLOMP
TMP
THUDD THUDD
KRR-SPLOOSH

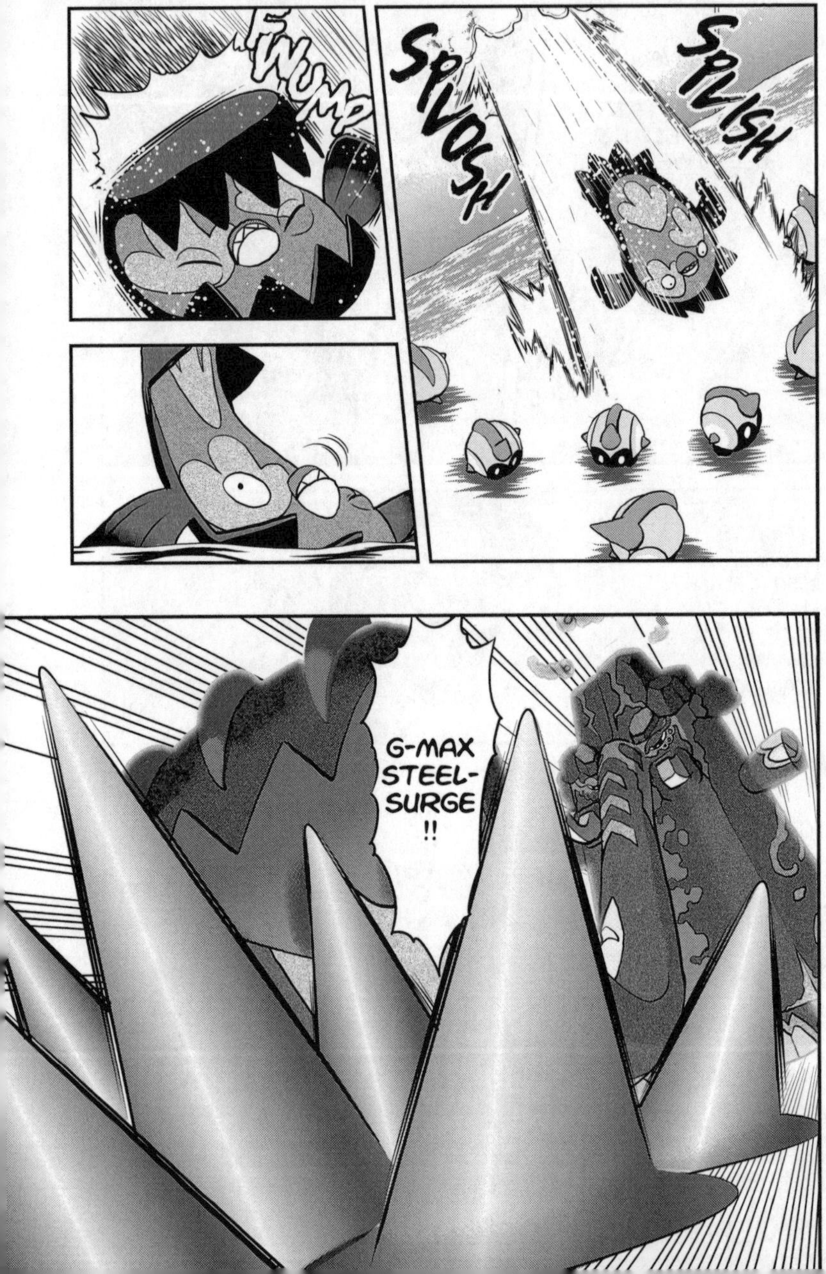
SPLISH
SPLVOSH
FWUMP
G-MAX STEEL-SURGE !!

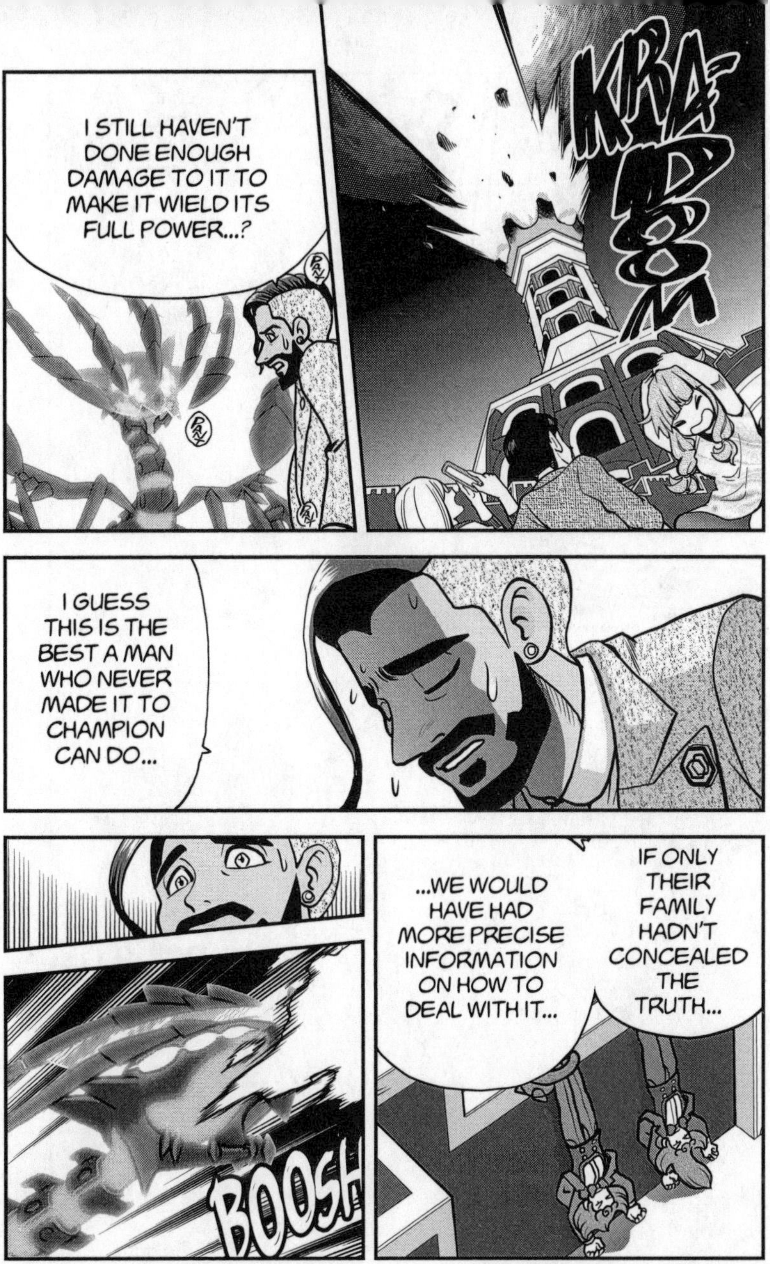
KRA-BOOM
I STILL HAVEN'T DONE ENOUGH DAMAGE TO IT TO MAKE IT WIELD ITS FULL POWER...?
I GUESS THIS IS THE BEST A MAN WHO NEVER MADE IT TO CHAMPION CAN DO...
IF ONLY THEIR FAMILY HADN'T CONCEALED THE TRUTH...
...WE WOULD HAVE HAD MORE PRECISE INFORMATION ON HOW TO DEAL WITH IT...
BOOSH

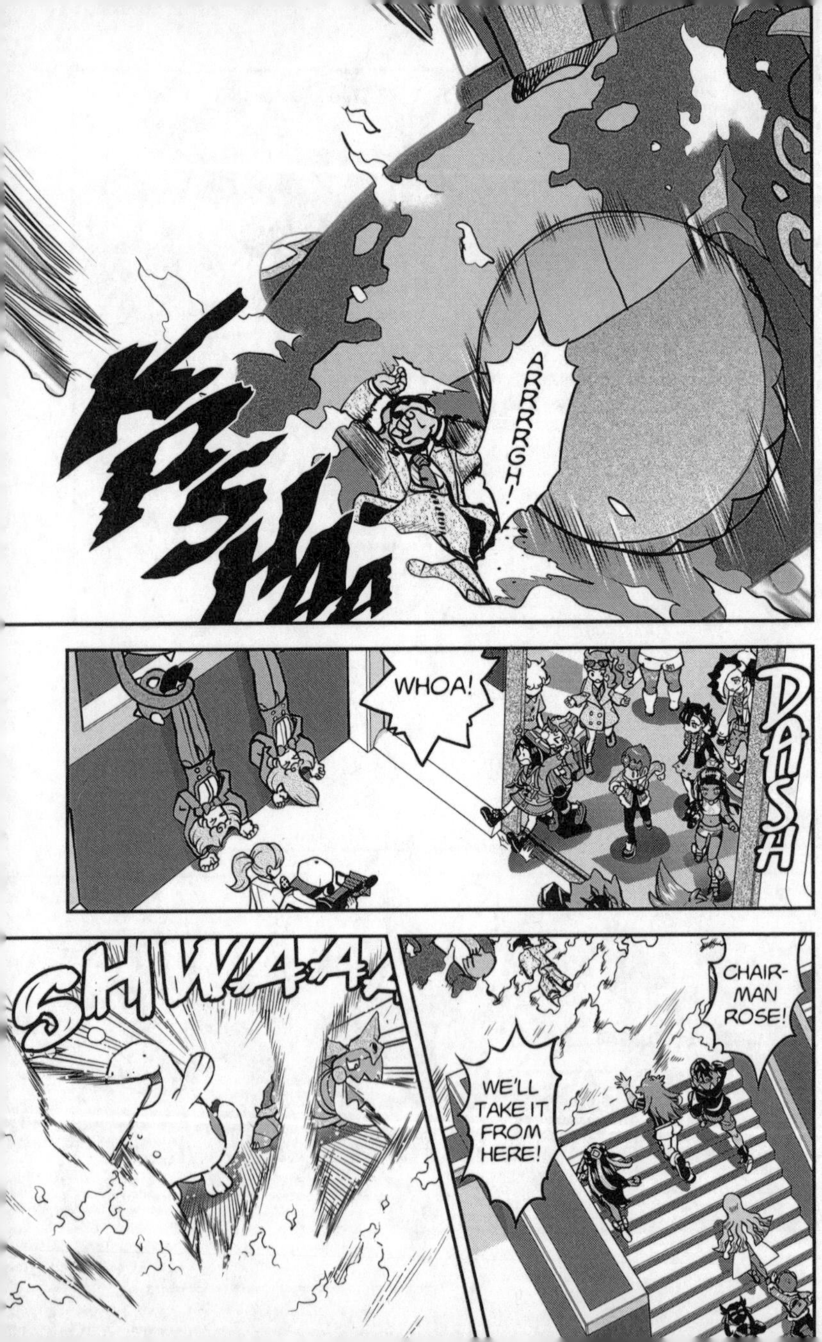
ARRRRGH!
DASH
WHOA!
CHAIR-
MAN
ROSE!
WE'LL
TAKE IT
FROM
HERE!
SHWAA

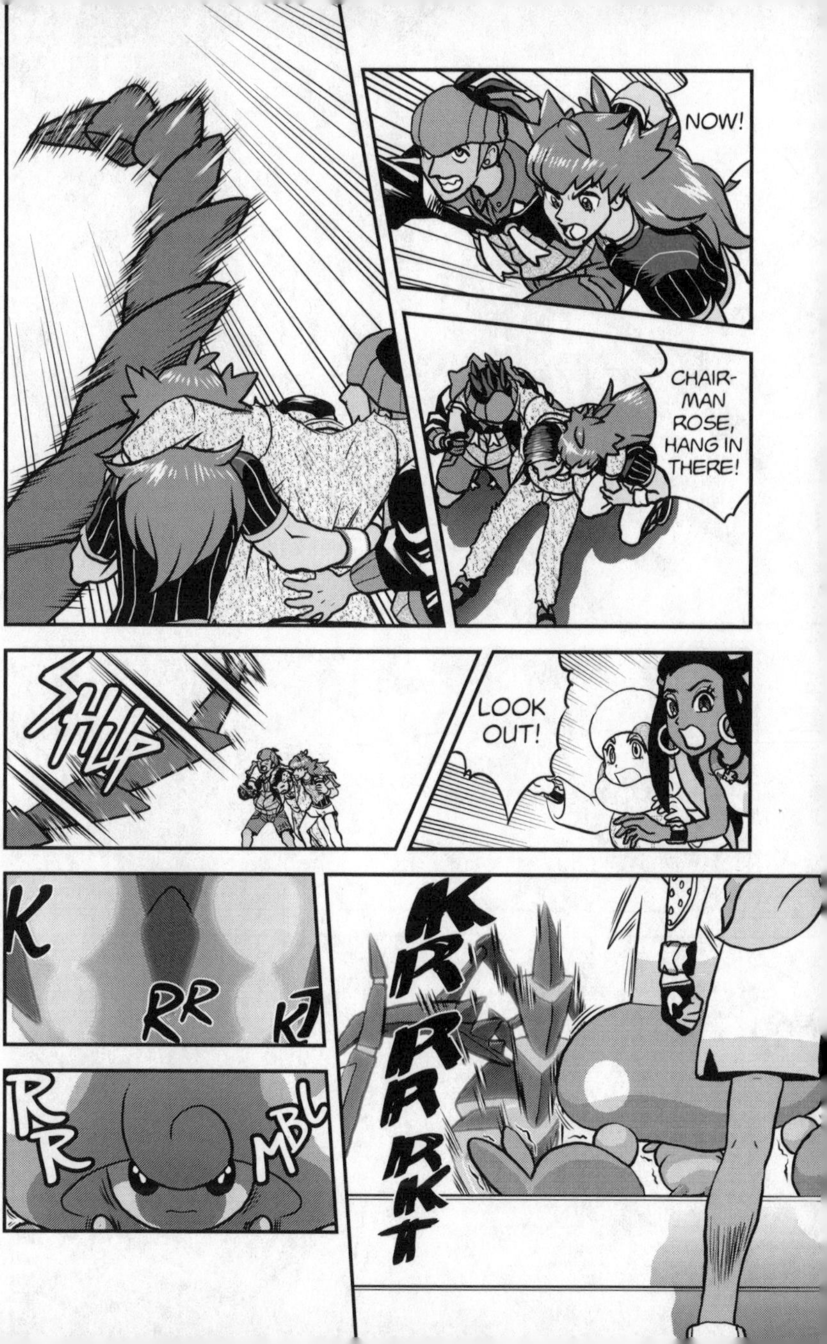
NOW!
CHAIR-MAN ROSE, HANG IN THERE!
LOOK OUT!
SHLP
KRRRRRKT
K
RR
KT
RR
MBL

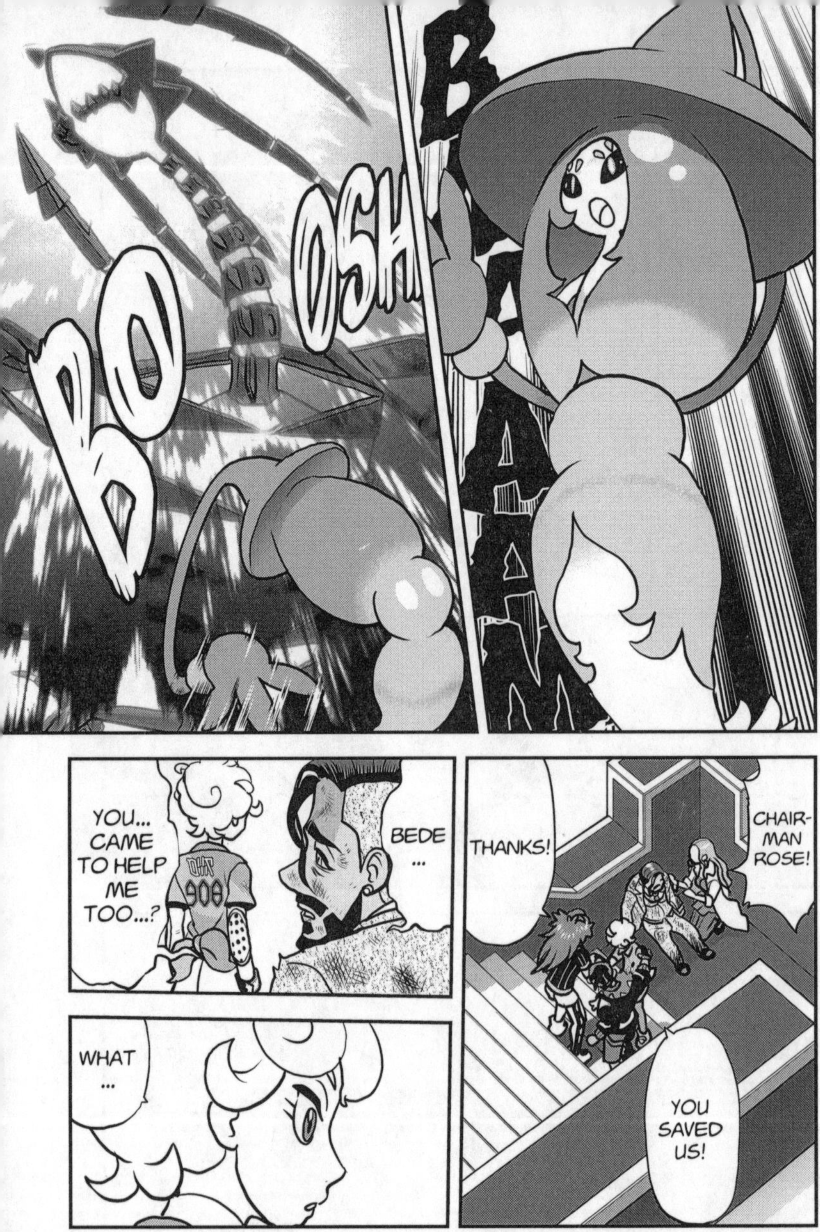

BAAAM
BOOSH
CHAIR-MAN ROSE!
THANKS!
YOU SAVED US!
BEDE ...
YOU... CAME TO HELP ME TOO...?
WHAT ...

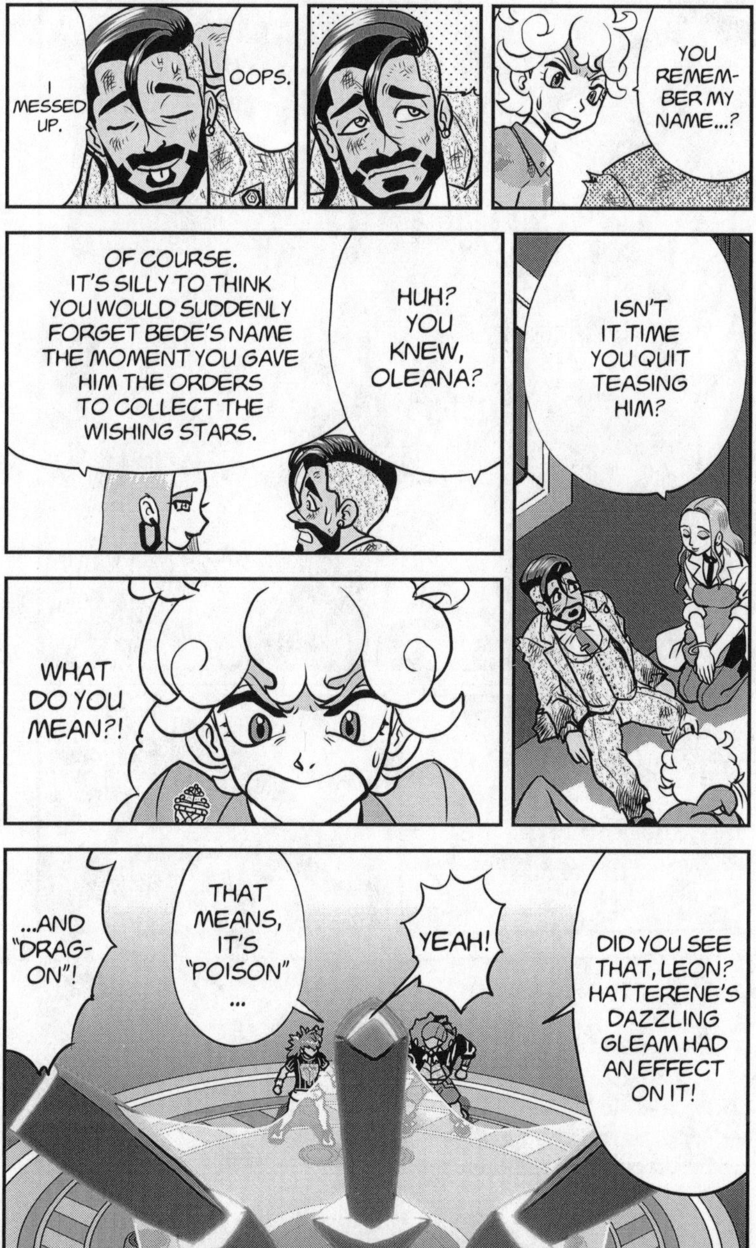
YOU REMEMBER MY NAME...?
OOPS.
I MESSED UP.
ISN'T IT TIME YOU QUIT TEASING HIM?
HUH? YOU KNEW, OLEANA?
OF COURSE. IT'S SILLY TO THINK YOU WOULD SUDDENLY FORGET BEDE'S NAME THE MOMENT YOU GAVE HIM THE ORDERS TO COLLECT THE WISHING STARS.
WHAT DO YOU MEAN?!
DID YOU SEE THAT, LEON? HATTERENE'S DAZZLING GLEAM HAD AN EFFECT ON IT!
YEAH!
THAT MEANS, IT'S "POISON"...
...AND "DRAG-ON"!

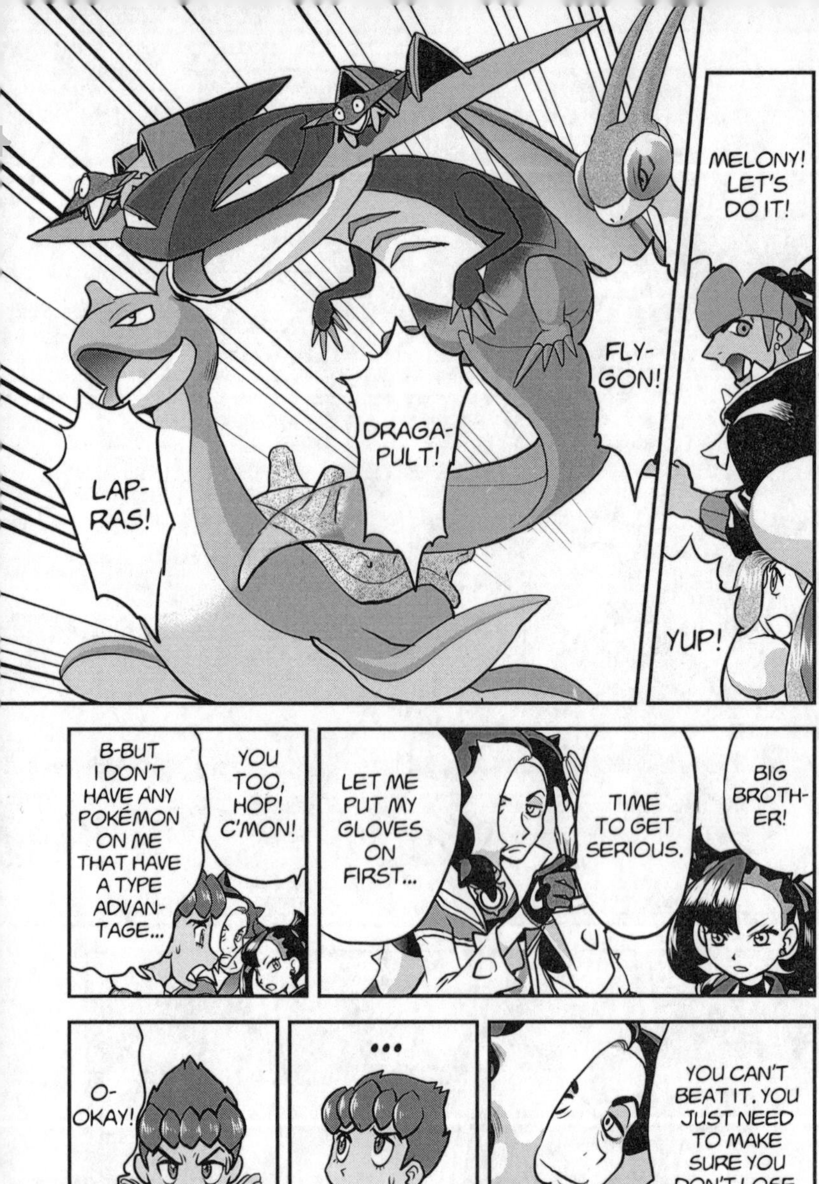
MELONY! LET'S DO IT!
YUP!
FLY-GON!
DRAGA-PULT!
LAP-RAS!
BIG BROTH-ER!
TIME TO GET SERIOUS.
LET ME PUT MY GLOVES ON FIRST...
YOU TOO, HOP! C'MON!
B-BUT I DON'T HAVE ANY POKÉMON ON ME THAT HAVE A TYPE ADVAN-TAGE...
YOU CAN'T BEAT IT. YOU JUST NEED TO MAKE SURE YOU DON'T LOSE.
...
O-OKAY!

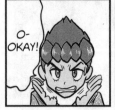

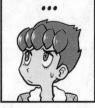

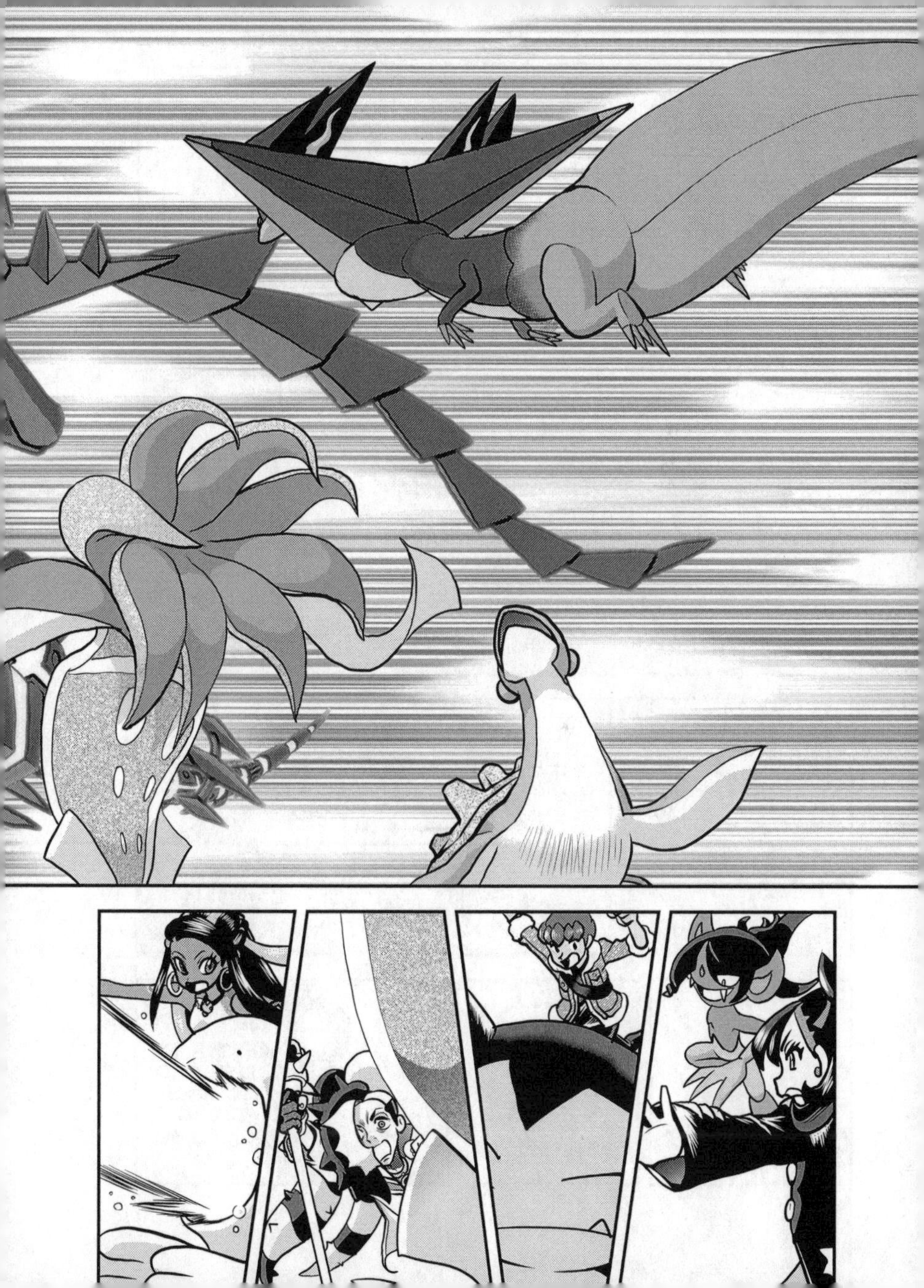

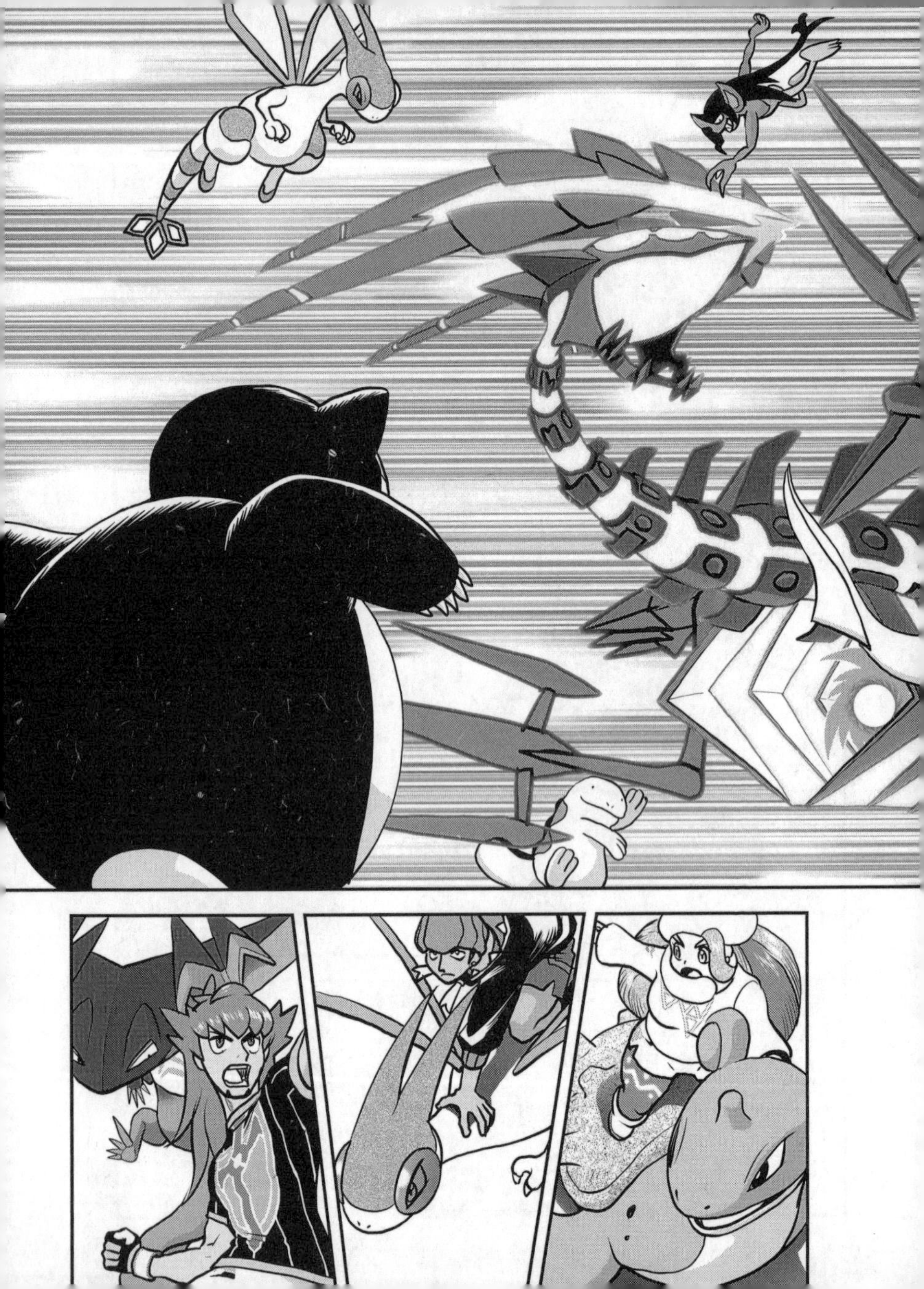

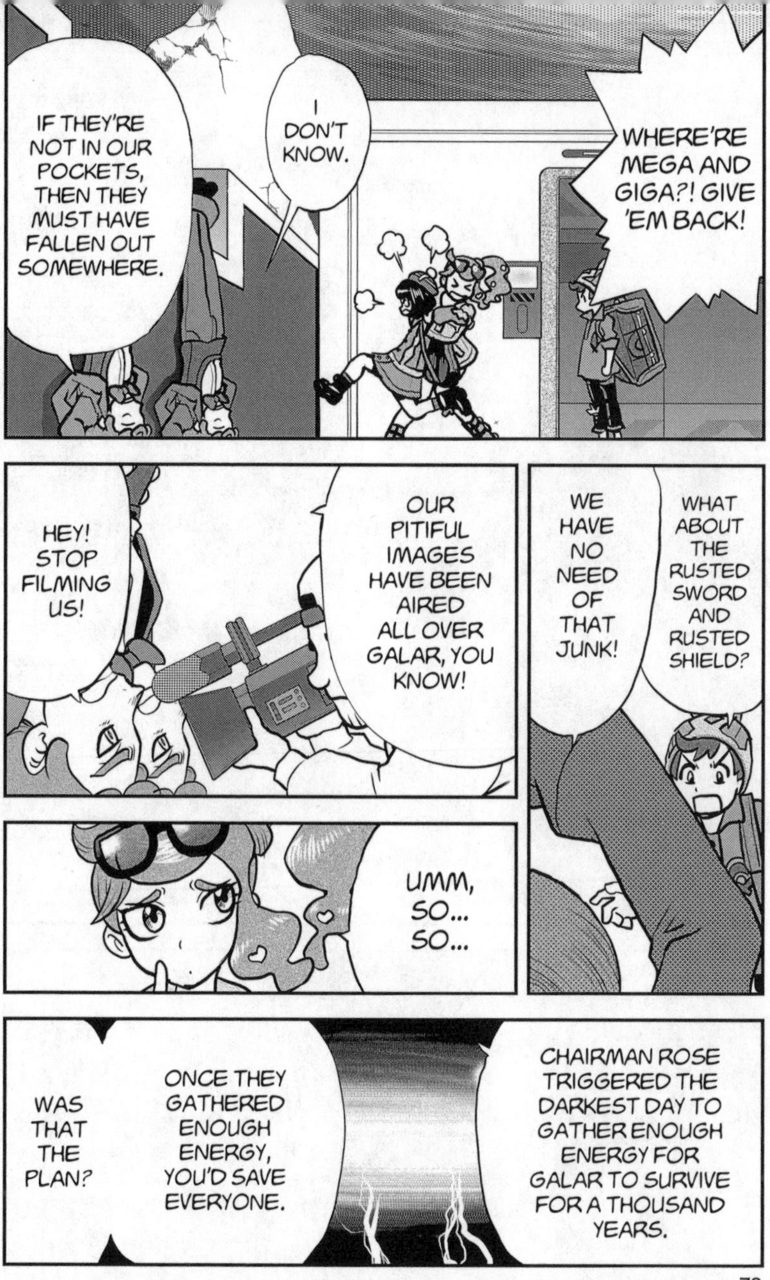
WHERE'RE MEGA AND GIGA?! GIVE 'EM BACK!
I DON'T KNOW.
IF THEY'RE NOT IN OUR POCKETS, THEN THEY MUST HAVE FALLEN OUT SOMEWHERE.
WHAT ABOUT THE RUSTED SWORD AND RUSTED SHIELD?
WE HAVE NO NEED OF THAT JUNK!
HEY! STOP FILMING US!
OUR PITIFUL IMAGES HAVE BEEN AIRED ALL OVER GALAR, YOU KNOW!
UMM, SO... SO...
CHAIRMAN ROSE TRIGGERED THE DARKEST DAY TO GATHER ENOUGH ENERGY FOR GALAR TO SURVIVE FOR A THOUSAND YEARS.
ONCE THEY GATHERED ENOUGH ENERGY, YOU'D SAVE EVERYONE.
WAS THAT THE PLAN?

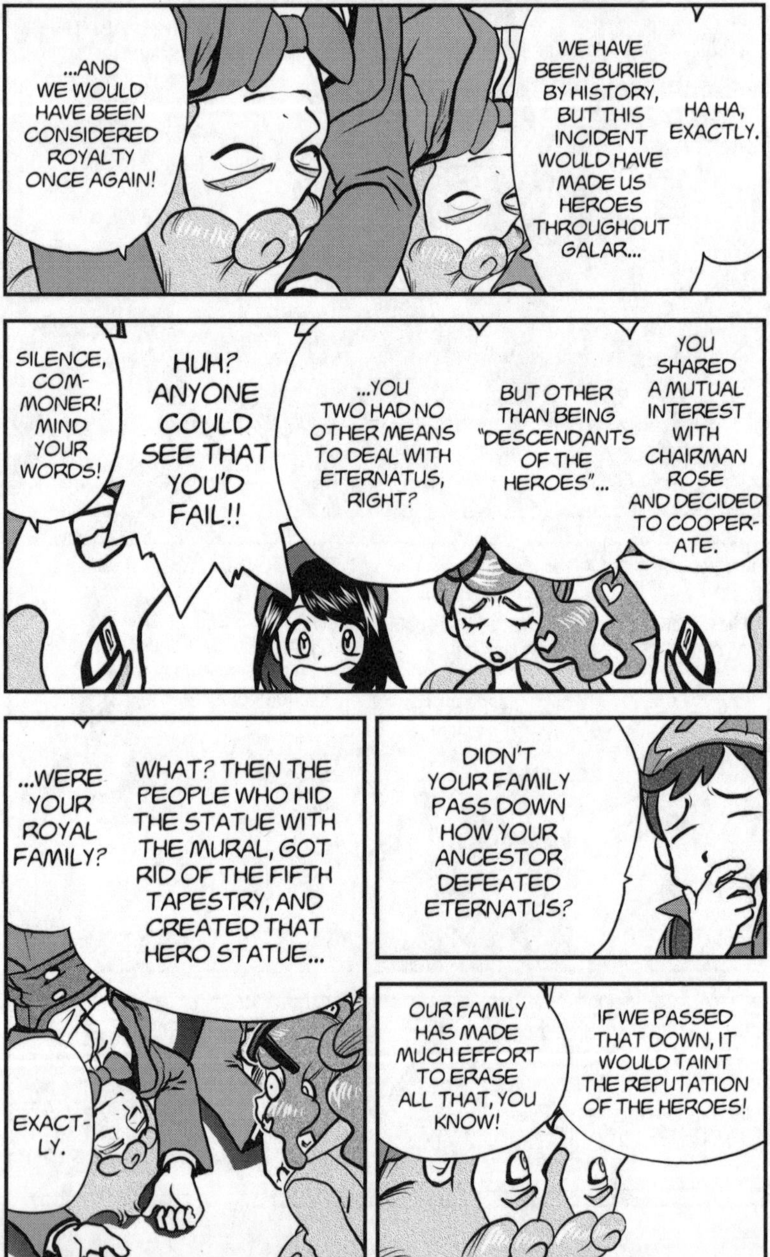
HA HA, EXACTLY.
WE HAVE BEEN BURIED BY HISTORY, BUT THIS INCIDENT WOULD HAVE MADE US HEROES THROUGHOUT GALAR...
...AND WE WOULD HAVE BEEN CONSIDERED ROYALTY ONCE AGAIN!
YOU SHARED A MUTUAL INTEREST WITH CHAIRMAN ROSE AND DECIDED TO COOPERATE.
BUT OTHER THAN BEING "DESCENDANTS OF THE HEROES"...
...YOU TWO HAD NO OTHER MEANS TO DEAL WITH ETERNATUS, RIGHT?
HUH? ANYONE COULD SEE THAT YOU'D FAIL!!
SILENCE, COM-MONER! MIND YOUR WORDS!
DIDN'T YOUR FAMILY PASS DOWN HOW YOUR ANCESTOR DEFEATED ETERNATUS?
IF WE PASSED THAT DOWN, IT WOULD TAINT THE REPUTATION OF THE HEROES!
OUR FAMILY HAS MADE MUCH EFFORT TO ERASE ALL THAT, YOU KNOW!
WHAT? THEN THE PEOPLE WHO HID THE STATUE WITH THE MURAL, GOT RID OF THE FIFTH TAPESTRY, AND CREATED THAT HERO STATUE...
...WERE YOUR ROYAL FAMILY?
EXACT-LY.

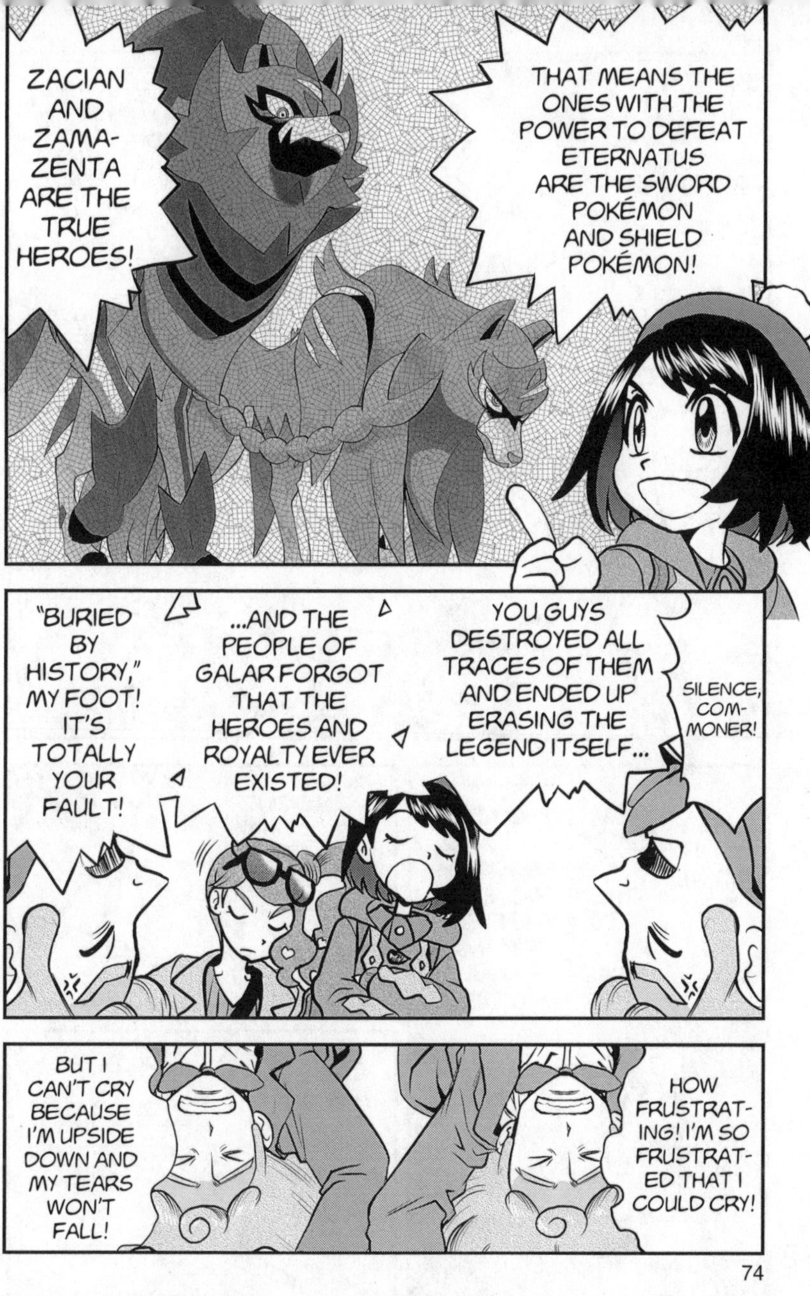
THAT MEANS THE ONES WITH THE POWER TO DEFEAT ETERNATUS ARE THE SWORD POKÉMON AND SHIELD POKÉMON!
ZACIAN AND ZAMA-ZENTA ARE THE TRUE HEROES!
YOU GUYS DESTROYED ALL TRACES OF THEM AND ENDED UP ERASING THE LEGEND ITSELF...
...AND THE PEOPLE OF GALAR FORGOT THAT THE HEROES AND ROYALTY EVER EXISTED!
"BURIED BY HISTORY," MY FOOT! IT'S TOTALLY YOUR FAULT!
SILENCE, COM-MONER!
HOW FRUSTRAT-ING! I'M SO FRUSTRAT-ED THAT I COULD CRY!
BUT I CAN'T CRY BECAUSE I'M UPSIDE DOWN AND MY TEARS WON'T FALL!

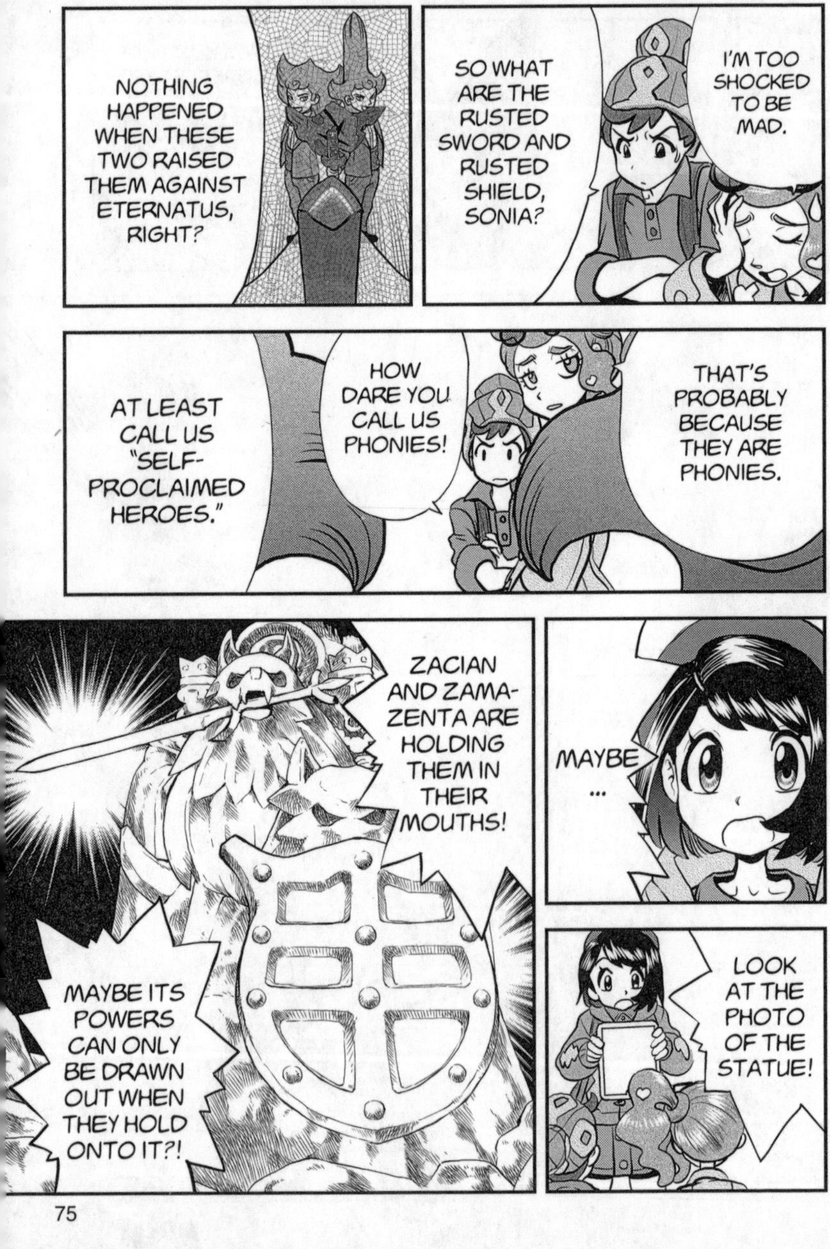
I'M TOO SHOCKED TO BE MAD.
SO WHAT ARE THE RUSTED SWORD AND RUSTED SHIELD, SONIA?
NOTHING HAPPENED WHEN THESE TWO RAISED THEM AGAINST ETERNATUS, RIGHT?
THAT'S PROBABLY BECAUSE THEY ARE PHONIES.
HOW DARE YOU CALL US PHONIES!
AT LEAST CALL US "SELF-PROCLAIMED HEROES."
MAYBE...
LOOK AT THE PHOTO OF THE STATUE!
ZACIAN AND ZAMAZENTA ARE HOLDING THEM IN THEIR MOUTHS!
MAYBE ITS POWERS CAN ONLY BE DRAWN OUT WHEN THEY HOLD ONTO IT?!

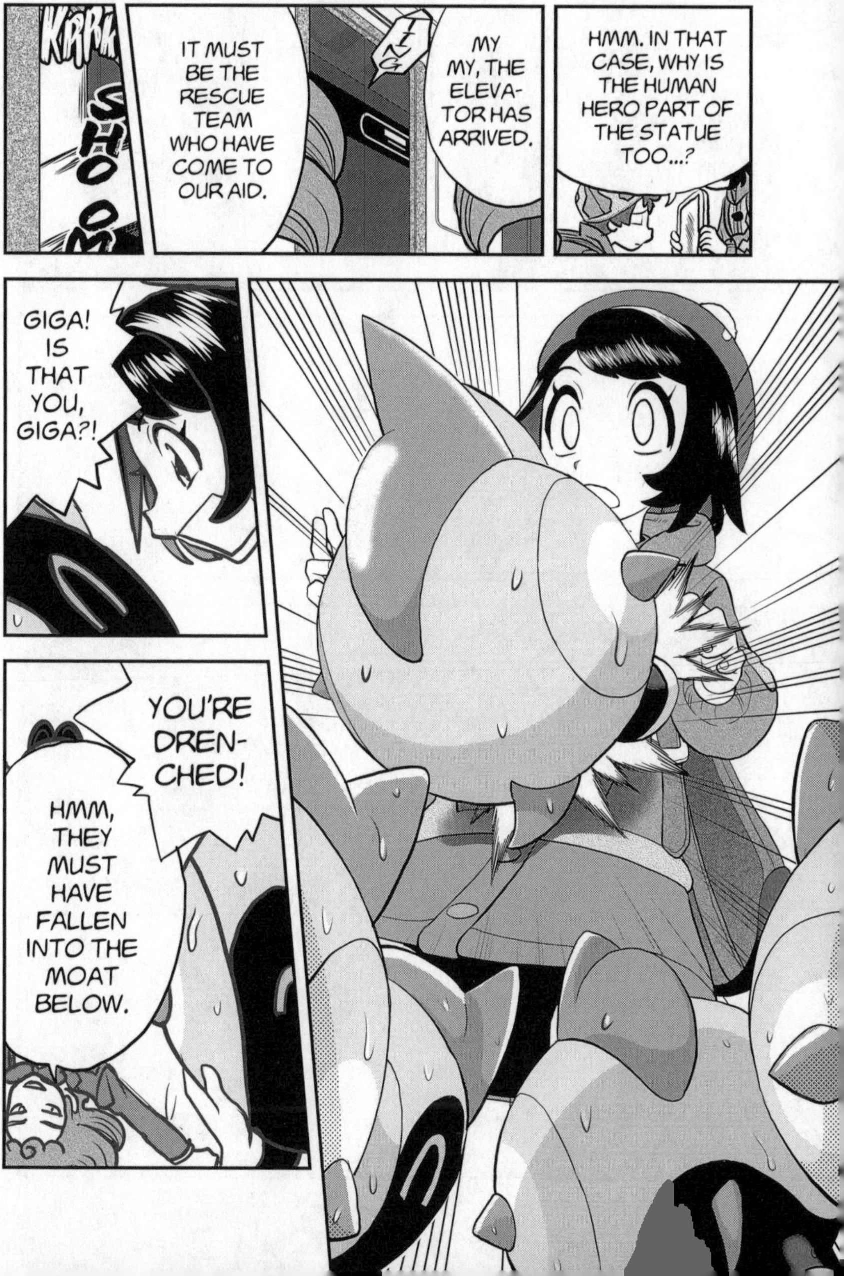
HMM. IN THAT CASE, WHY IS THE HUMAN HERO PART OF THE STATUE TOO...?
MY MY, THE ELEVATOR HAS ARRIVED.
TING
IT MUST BE THE RESCUE TEAM WHO HAVE COME TO OUR AID.
KRRK
SHOOOM
GIGA! IS THAT YOU, GIGA?!
YOU'RE DRENCHED!
HMM, THEY MUST HAVE FALLEN INTO THE MOAT BELOW.

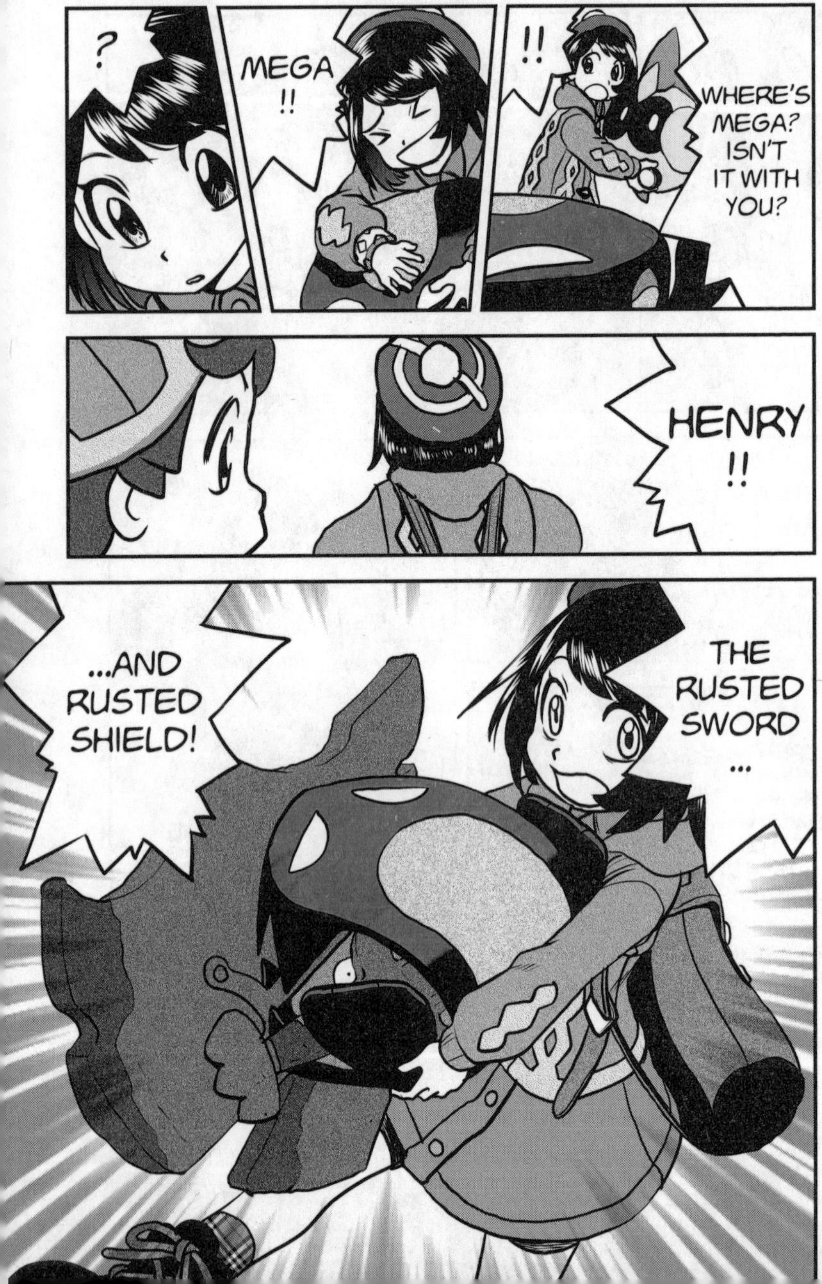
!!
WHERE'S MEGA? ISN'T IT WITH YOU?
MEGA !!
?
HENRY !!
THE RUSTED SWORD ...
...AND RUSTED SHIELD!

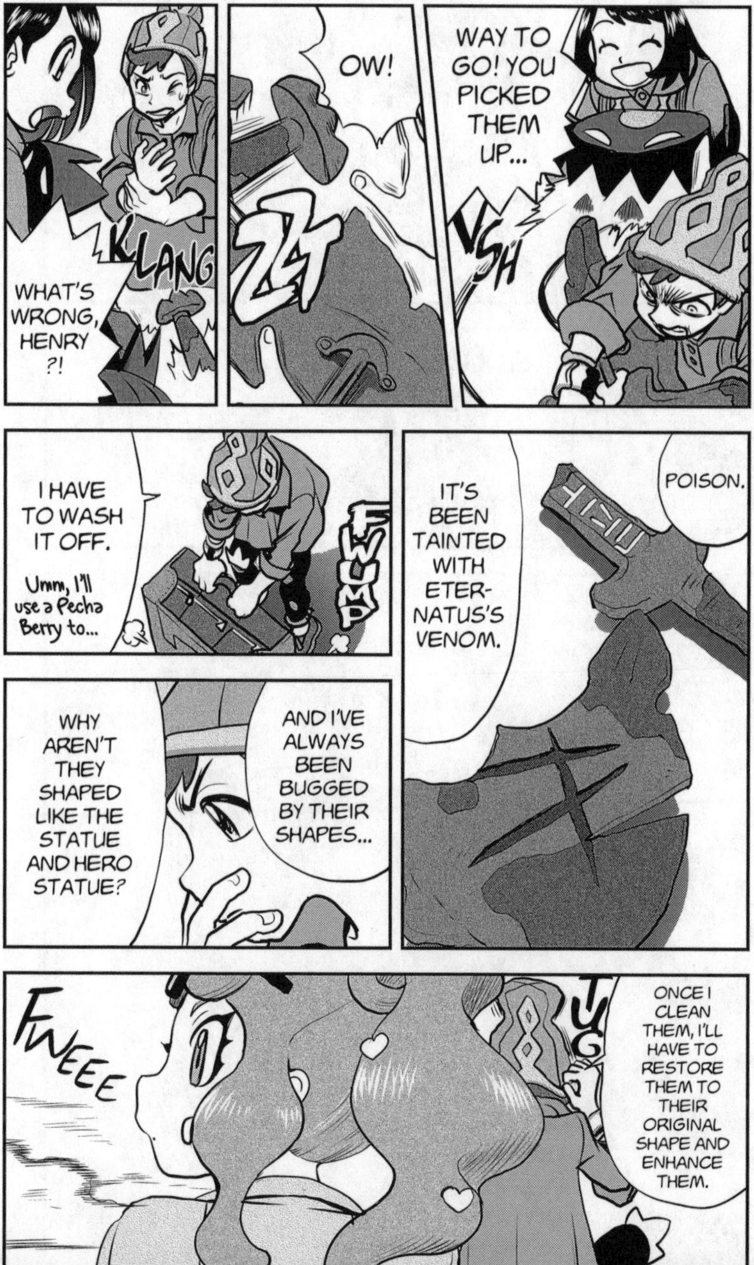
WAY TO GO! YOU PICKED THEM UP...
VSH
OW!
KLANG
WHAT'S WRONG, HENRY ?!
POISON.
IT'S BEEN TAINTED WITH ETER-NATUS'S VENOM.
I HAVE TO WASH IT OFF.
Umm, I'll use a Pecha Berry to...
FWUMP
AND I'VE ALWAYS BEEN BUGGED BY THEIR SHAPES...
WHY AREN'T THEY SHAPED LIKE THE STATUE AND HERO STATUE?
TUG
ONCE I CLEAN THEM, I'LL HAVE TO RESTORE THEM TO THEIR ORIGINAL SHAPE AND ENHANCE THEM.
FWEEEE

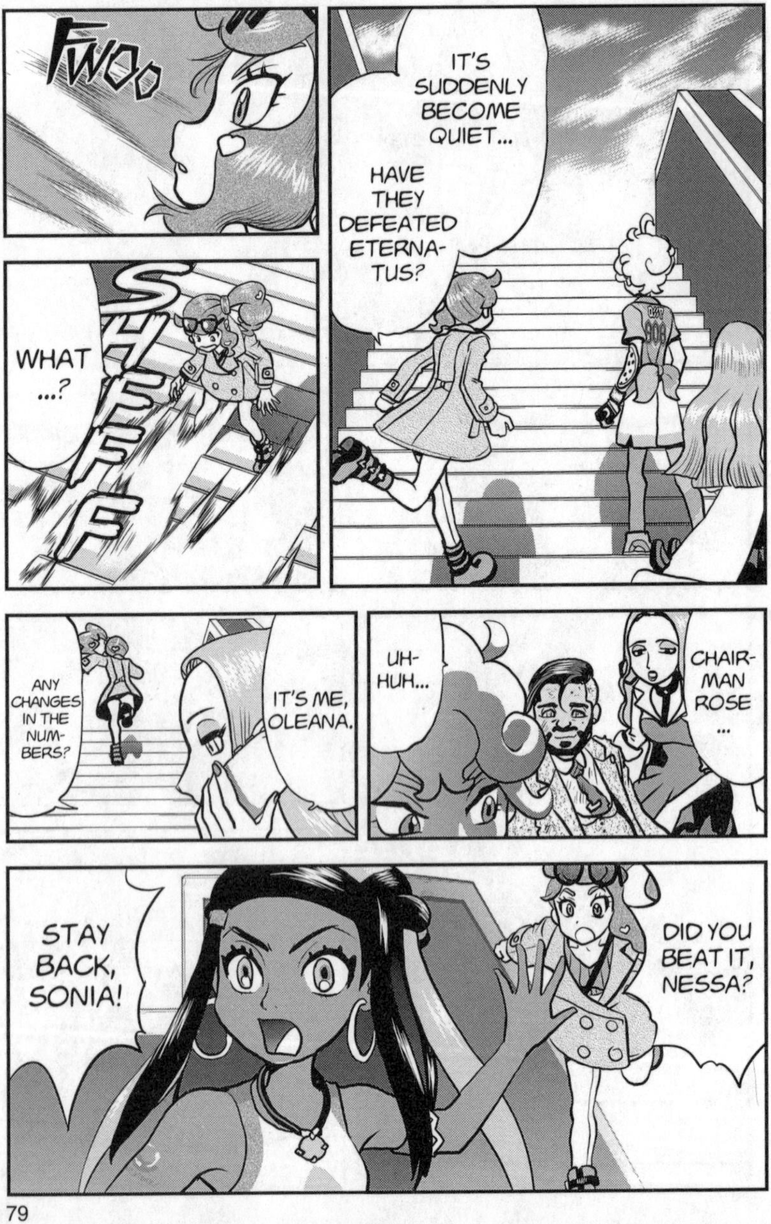
IT'S SUDDENLY BECOME QUIET...
HAVE THEY DEFEATED ETERNA-TUS?
FWOO
SHFFFF
WHAT ...?
CHAIR-MAN ROSE ...
UH-HUH...
IT'S ME, OLEANA.
ANY CHANGES IN THE NUM-BERS?
DID YOU BEAT IT, NESSA?
STAY BACK, SONIA!

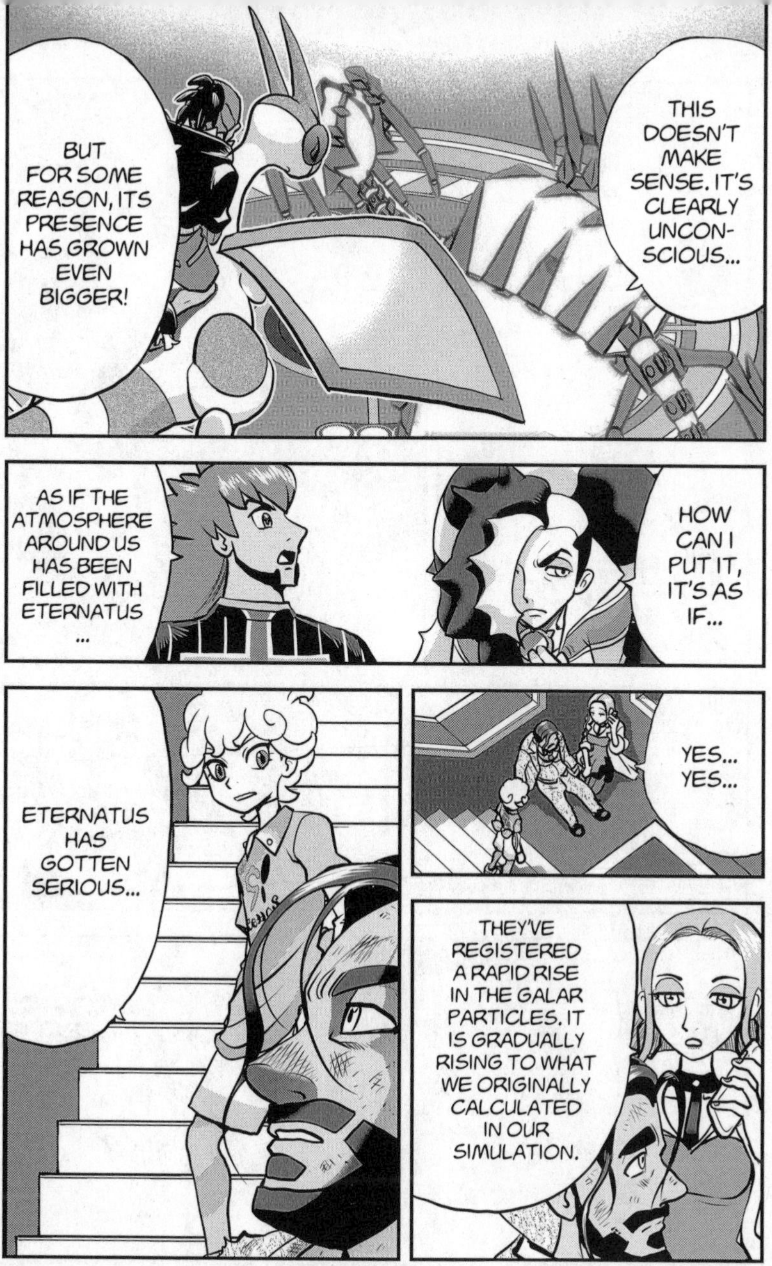
THIS DOESN'T MAKE SENSE. IT'S CLEARLY UNCONSCIOUS...
BUT FOR SOME REASON, ITS PRESENCE HAS GROWN EVEN BIGGER!
HOW CAN I PUT IT, IT'S AS IF...
AS IF THE ATMOSPHERE AROUND US HAS BEEN FILLED WITH ETERNATUS...
YES... YES...
THEY'VE REGISTERED A RAPID RISE IN THE GALAR PARTICLES. IT IS GRADUALLY RISING TO WHAT WE ORIGINALLY CALCULATED IN OUR SIMULATION.
ETERNATUS HAS GOTTEN SERIOUS...

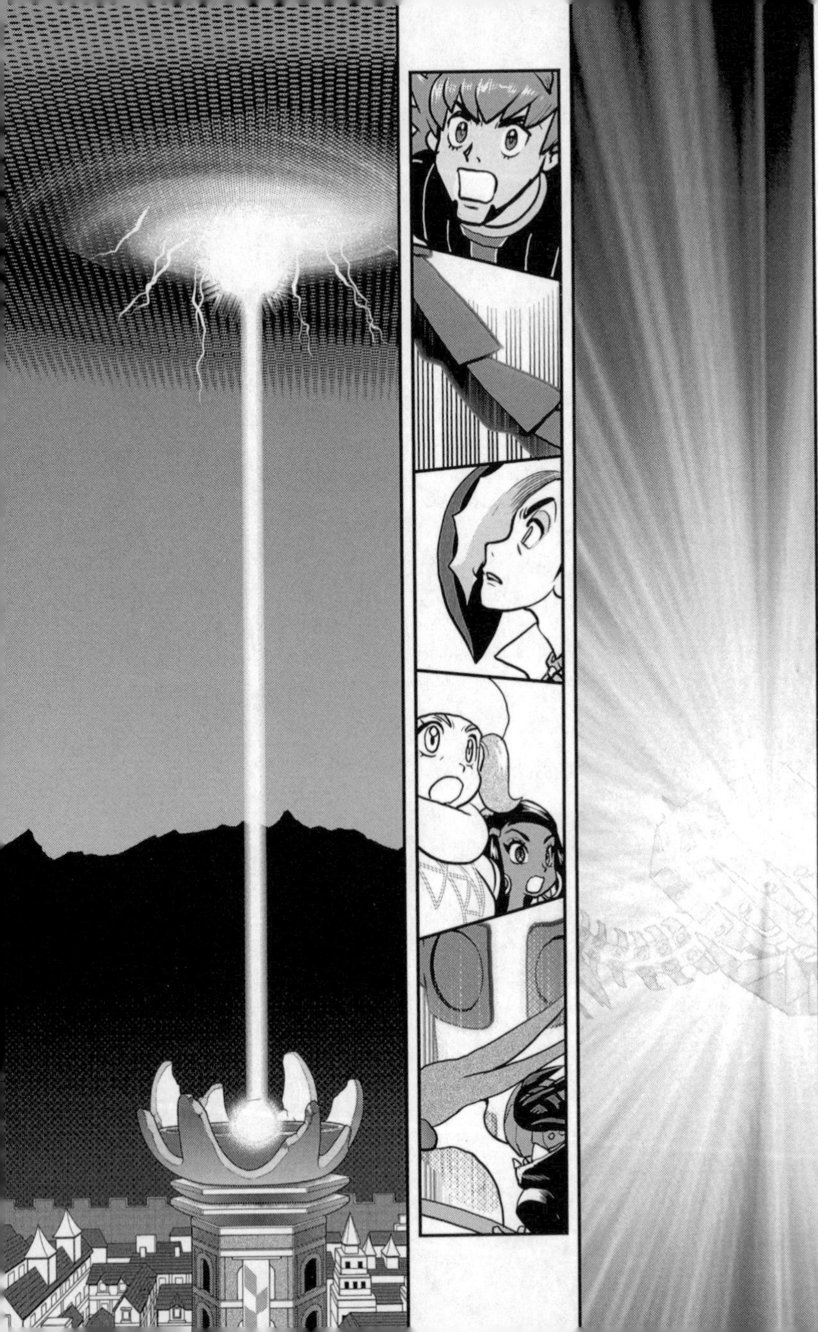

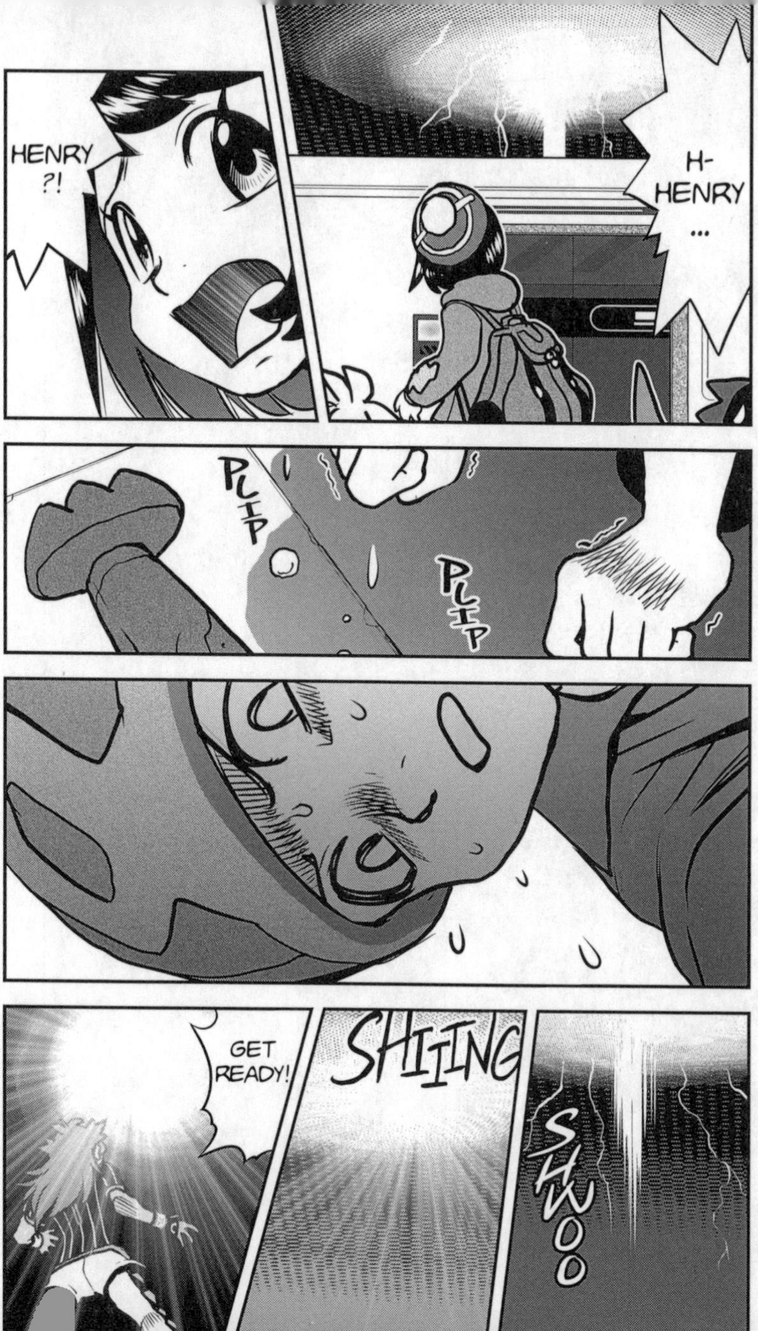
H- HENRY ...
HENRY ?!
PLIP
PLIP
SHWOO
SHIIING
GET READY!

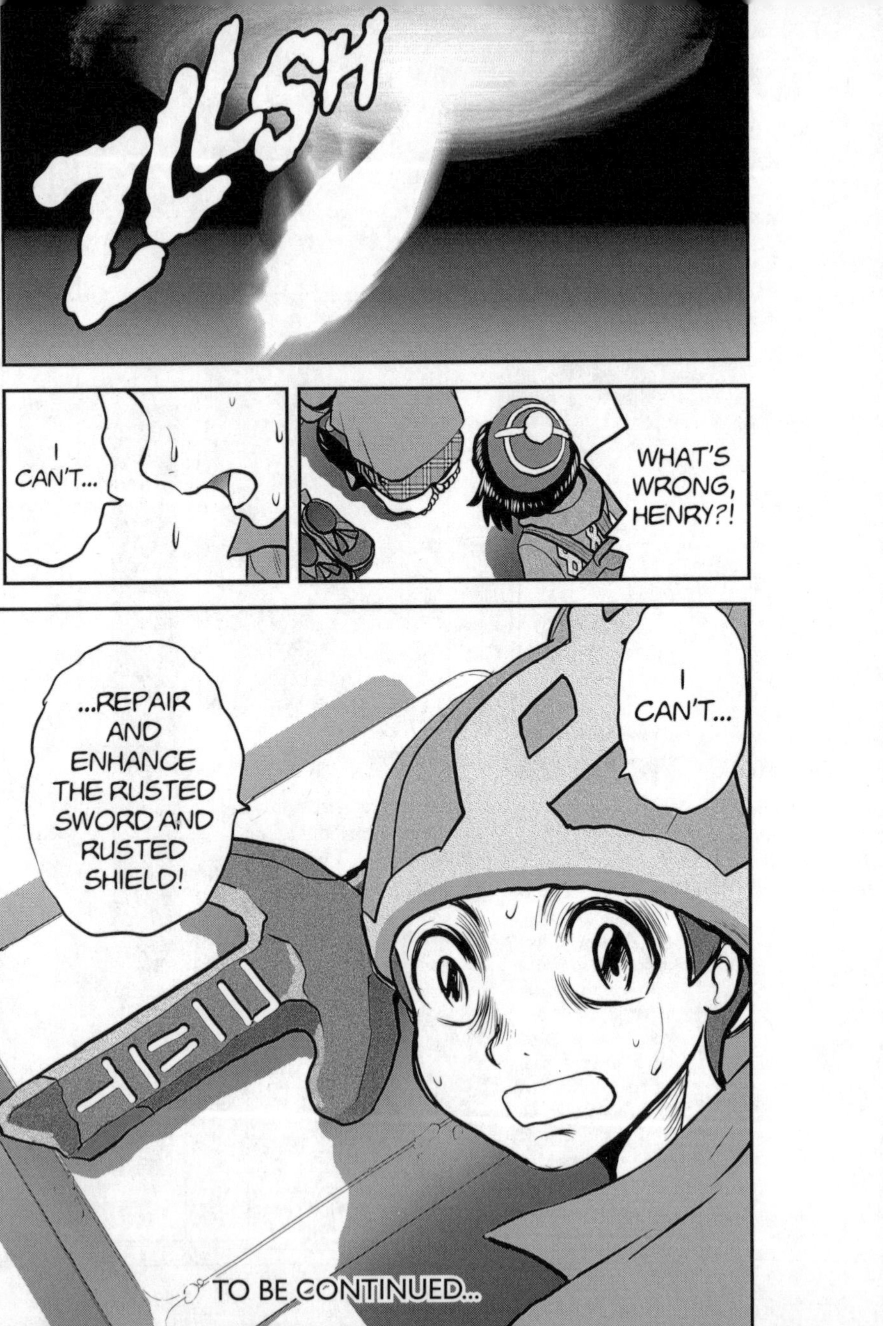
ZLSH
WHAT'S WRONG, HENRY?!
I CAN'T...
I CAN'T...
...REPAIR AND ENHANCE THE RUSTED SWORD AND RUSTED SHIELD!
TO BE CONTINUED...

GIGANTAMAX COALOSSAL

TYPE	Rock, Fire
ABILITY	Steam Engine Flame Body
G-MAX MOVE	G-Max Volcalith

HEIGHT	137'10"+
WEIGHT	??? lbs

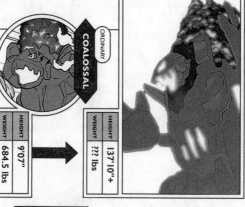

ORDINARY

COALOSSAL

HEIGHT	9'07"
WEIGHT	684.5 lbs

Coalossal turns into a giant, fearsome shape that scatters coal from its head. It may look intimidating, but there is a heartwarming story that claims it once saved many people from a harsh cold wave by serving as a giant stove!!

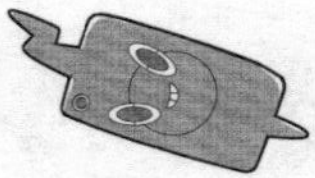

STRATEGY NOTES

The Rock-type move used by a Gigantamax Coalossal is G-Max Volcalith. It's a move that will repeatedly deal damage to its opponent, so you will need to endure its attacks. G-Max Volcalith is a move aimed towards those other than Rock types, so if your Pokémon is a Rock type, it will nullify the attack.

Hidenori Kusaka is the writer for *Pokémon Adventures*. Running continuously for over 25 years, *Pokémon Adventures* is the only manga series to completely cover all the *Pokémon* games and has become one of the most popular series of all time. In addition to writing manga, he also edits children's books and plans mixed-media projects for Shogakukan's children's magazines. He uses the Pokémon Electrode as his author portrait.

———————

Satoshi Yamamoto is the artist for *Pokémon Adventures*, which he began working on in 2001, starting with volume 10. Yamamoto launched his manga career in 1993 with the horror-action title *Kimen Senshi*, which ran in Shogakukan's *Weekly Shonen Sunday* magazine, followed by the series *Kaze no Denshosha*. Yamamoto's favorite manga creators/artists include FUJIKO F FUJIO (*Doraemon*), Yukinobu Hoshino (*2001 Nights*), and Katsuhiro Otomo (*Akira*). He loves films, monsters, detective novels, and punk rock music. He uses the Pokémon Swalot as his artist portrait.

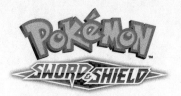

Pokémon: Sword & Shield
Volume 9
VIZ Media Edition

Story by HIDENORI KUSAKA
Art by SATOSHI YAMAMOTO

©2024 Pokémon.
©1995–2022 Nintendo / Creatures Inc. / GAME FREAK inc.
TM, ®, and character names are trademarks of Nintendo.
© 2020 Hidenori KUSAKA, Satoshi YAMAMOTO
All rights reserved.
Original Japanese edition published by SHOGAKUKAN.
English translation rights in the United States of America, Canada, the United Kingdom,
Ireland, Australia and New Zealand arranged with SHOGAKUKAN.

Original Cover Design—Hiroyuki KAWASOME (grafio)

Translation—Tetsuichiro Miyaki
English Adaptation—Molly Tanzer
Touch-Up & Lettering—Annaliese "Ace" Christman
Design—Alice Lewis
Editor—Joel Enos

Special thanks to Trish Ledoux and Wendy Hoover at The Pokémon Company International.

Printed in the U.S.A.

Published by VIZ Media, LLC
P.O. Box 77010
San Francisco, CA 94107

10 9 8 7 6 5 4 3 2 1
First printing, April 2024

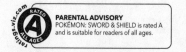

viz.com

Coming Next Volume

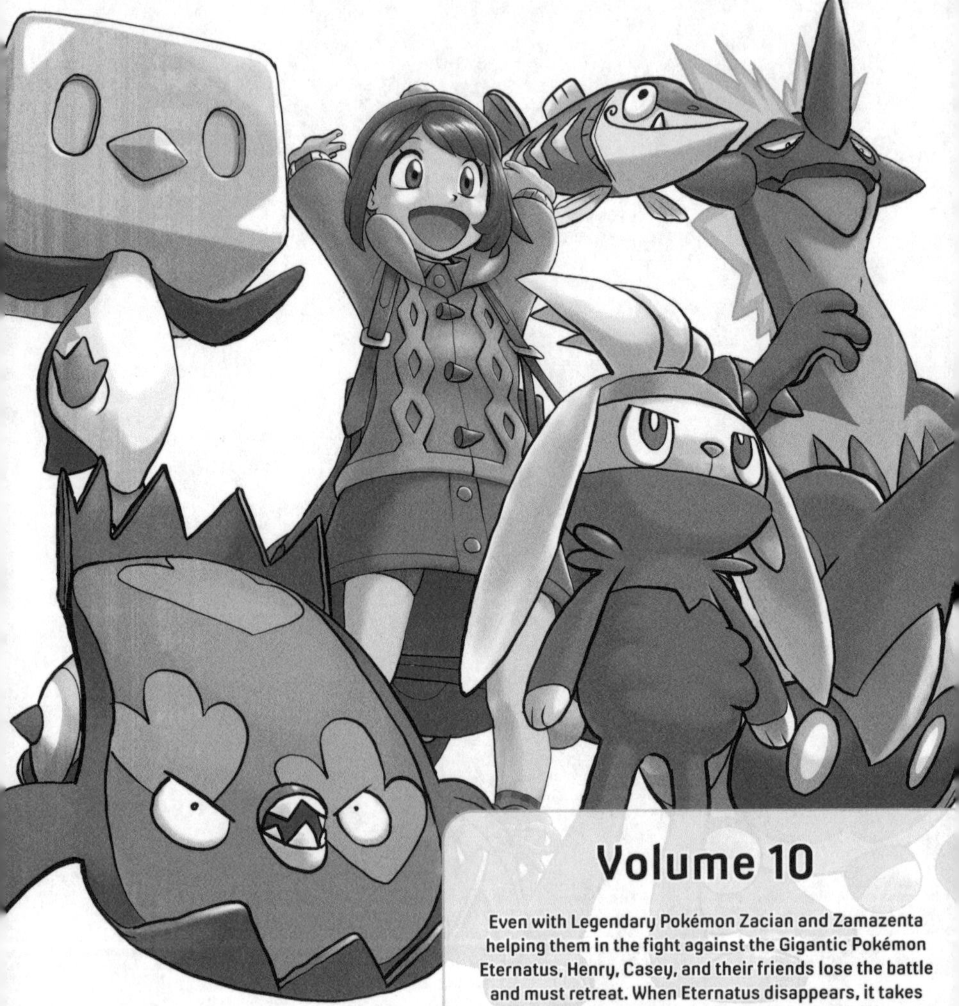

Volume 10

Even with Legendary Pokémon Zacian and Zamazenta helping them in the fight against the Gigantic Pokémon Eternatus, Henry, Casey, and their friends lose the battle and must retreat. When Eternatus disappears, it takes Henry, the Rusted Sword, and the Rusted Shield along for the ride! Can the team find and save Henry?!

THE ART OF

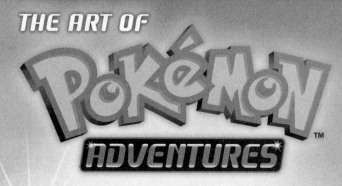

POKÉMON
ADVENTURES™

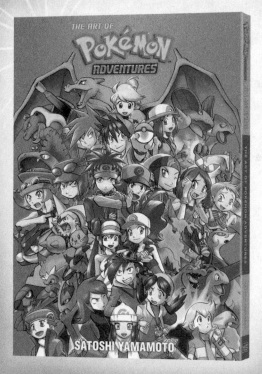

STORY AND ART BY
Satoshi Yamamoto

A collection of beautiful full-color art from the artist of the Pokémon Adventures graphic novel series! In addition to illustrations of your favorite Pokémon, this vibrant volume includes exclusive sketches and storyboards, four pull-out posters, and an exclusive manga side story!

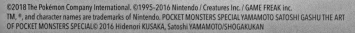

viz.com

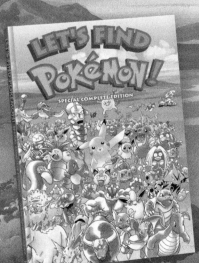

LET'S FIND POKÉMON!

SPECIAL COMPLETE EDITION

WHERE IS PIKACHU? FIND POKÉMON IN COLORFUL PICTURES OF PALLET TOWN, CELADON CITY AND OTHER SCENIC SPOTS FROM THE GAME!

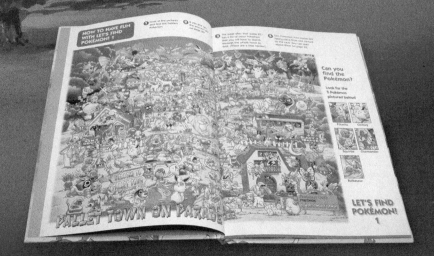

THREE *LET'S FIND* BOOKS COLLECTED IN ONE VOLUME!

VIZ

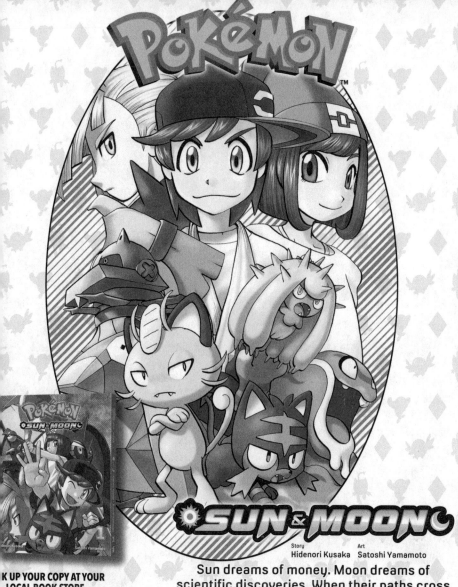

Pokémon

SUN & MOON

Story
Hidenori Kusaka

Art
Satoshi Yamamoto

Sun dreams of money. Moon dreams of
scientific discoveries. When their paths cross
with Team Skull, both their plans go awry...

K UP YOUR COPY AT YOUR
LOCAL BOOK STORE.

RATED A ALL AGES

IZ

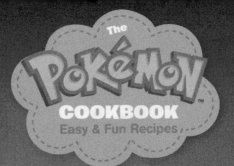

The Pokémon COOKBOOK
Easy & Fun Recipes

by Maki Kudo

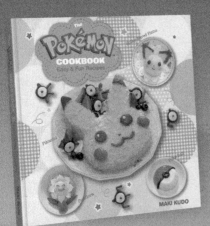

Create delicious dishes that look like your favorite Pokémon characters with more than 35 fun, easy recipes. Make a Poké Ball sushi roll, Pikachu ramen or mashed Meowth potatoes for your next party, weekend activity or powered-up lunch box.

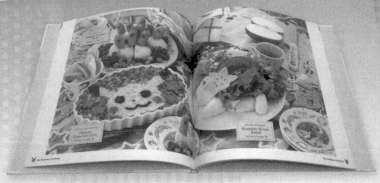

VIZ
viz.com

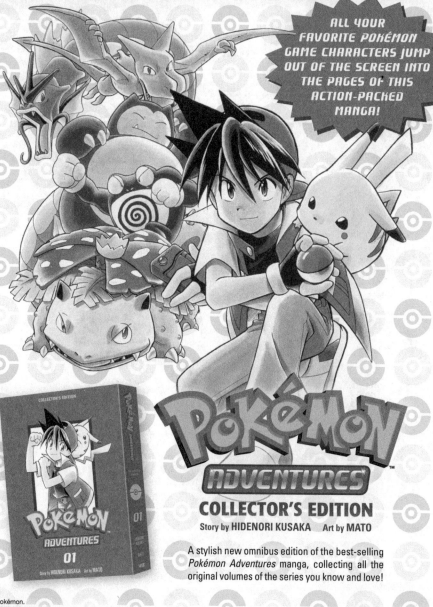

ALL YOUR FAVORITE POKÉMON GAME CHARACTERS JUMP OUT OF THE SCREEN INTO THE PAGES OF THIS ACTION-PACKED MANGA!

Pokémon
ADVENTURES
COLLECTOR'S EDITION
Story by HIDENORI KUSAKA   Art by MATO

A stylish new omnibus edition of the best-selling *Pokémon Adventures* manga, collecting all the original volumes of the series you know and love!

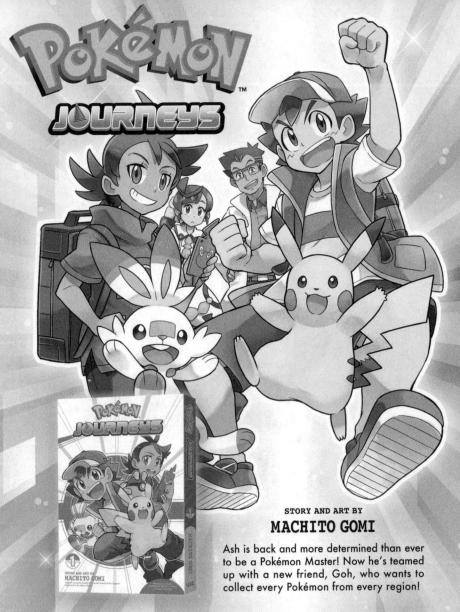

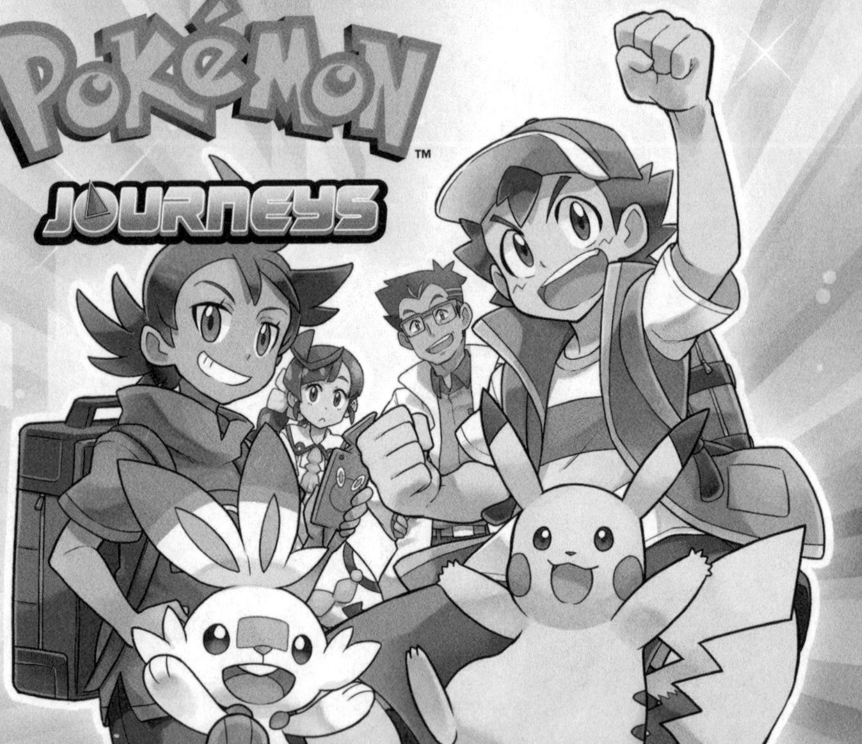
Pokémon™
Journeys

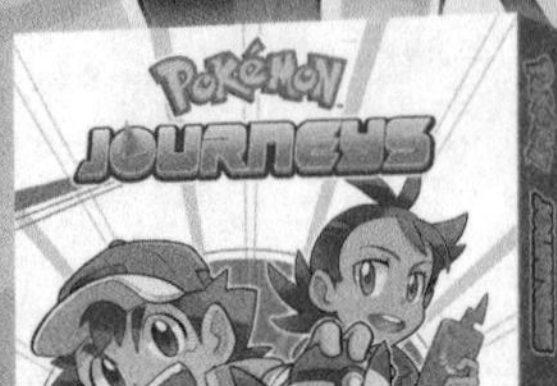
Pokémon
Journeys
1
STORY AND ART BY
MACHITO GOMI

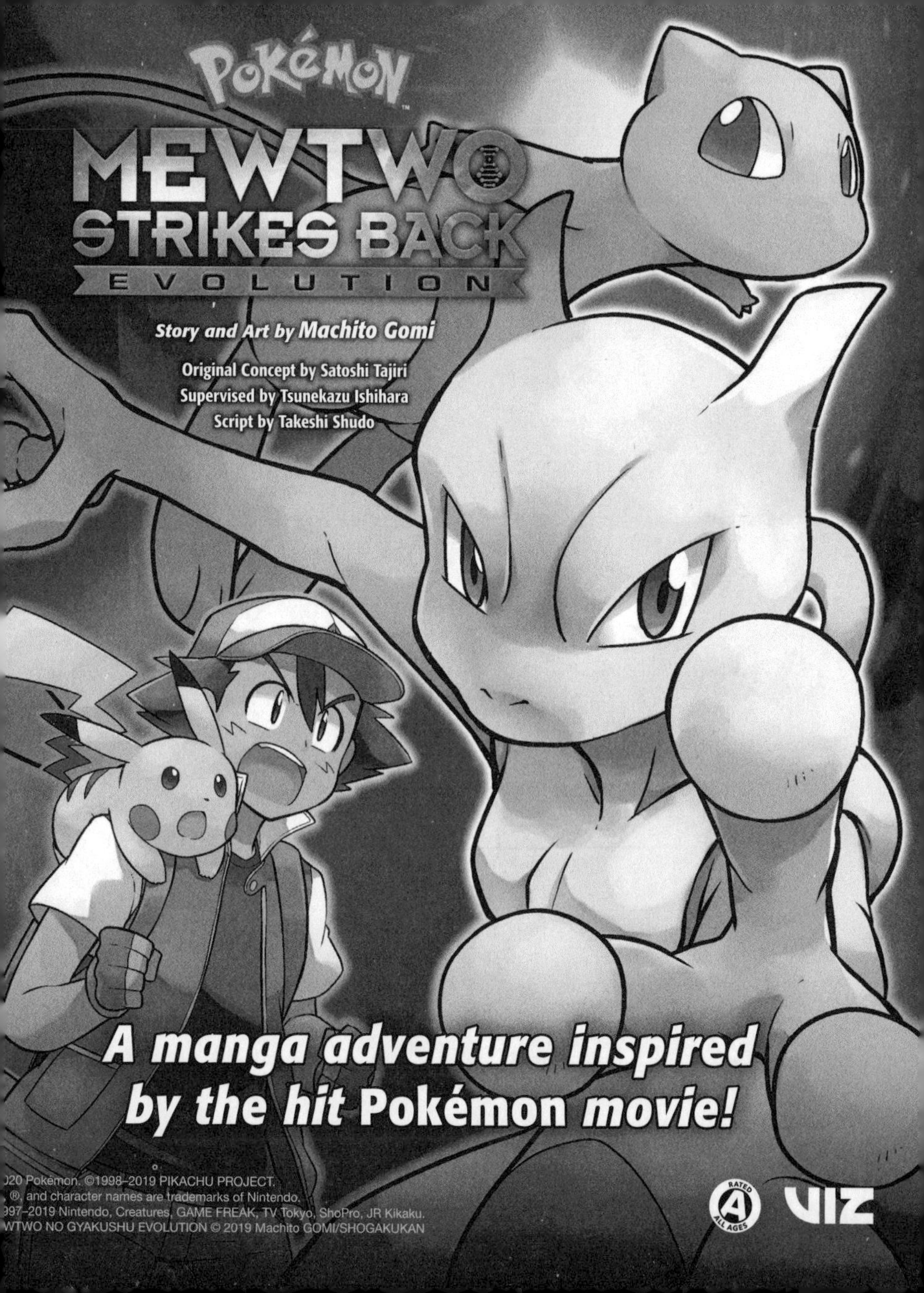

Pokémon

MEWTWO STRIKES BACK
EVOLUTION

Story and Art by **Machito Gomi**

Original Concept by Satoshi Tajiri
Supervised by Tsunekazu Ishihara
Script by Takeshi Shudo

A manga adventure inspired by the hit Pokémon movie!

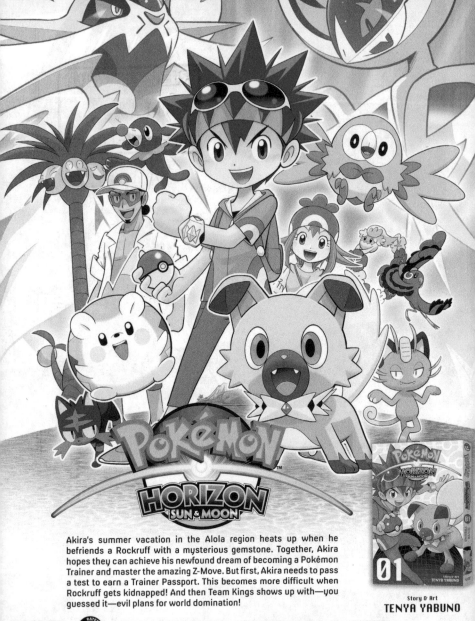

POKéMON

HORIZON
SUN & MOON

Akira's summer vacation in the Alola region heats up when he befriends a Rockruff with a mysterious gemstone. Together, Akira hopes they can achieve his newfound dream of becoming a Pokémon Trainer and master the amazing Z-Move. But first, Akira needs to pass a test to earn a Trainer Passport. This becomes more difficult when Rockruff gets kidnapped! And then Team Kings shows up with—you guessed it—evil plans for world domination!

Story & Art
TENYA YABUNO

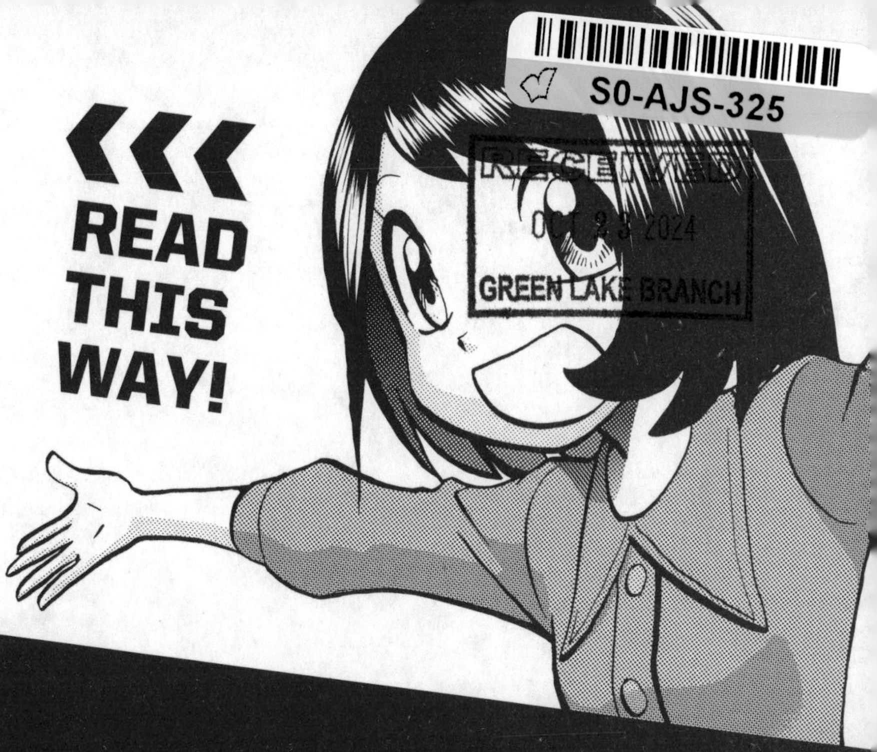
READ
THIS
WAY!

THIS IS THE END OF THIS GRAPHIC NOVEL!

To properly enjoy this VIZ Media graphic novel, please turn it around and begin reading from right to left.

This book has been printed in the original Japanese format in order to preserve the orientation of the original artwork. Have fun with it!

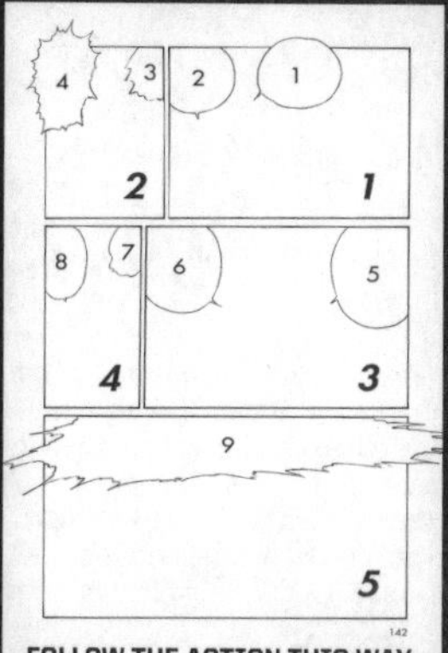

FOLLOW THE ACTION THIS WAY.